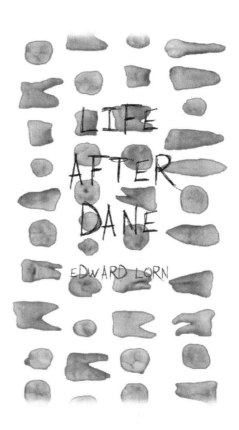

LIFE

AFTER

DANE

EDWARD LORN

Life After Dane

DEDICATION

For Barbara, Tamara, and Regina.

Also by Edward Lorn

Bay's End
Dastardly Bastard
Hope for the Wicked
Cruelty
Fog Warning
Pennies for the Damned
Fairy Lights
The Sound of Broken Ribs
The Bedding of Boys
Everything is Horrible How
No Home for Boys

Collections

What the Dark Brings
Others & Oddities
Word

"Happy families are all alike; every unhappy family is unhappy in its own way."
~*Anna Karenina*, by Leo Tolstoy

"Marley was dead: to begin with."
~*A Christmas Carol*, by Charles Dickens

ONE

THE STATE OF ARKANSAS PUT my son to sleep on October 25, 2013. All across the country, from Colorado to Virginia, forty-two families were finally able to rest. I knew those grieving souls by faces, not personalities. Their tears were familiar, yet their pain was not. I could recall their loved ones easily, as they were the victims. My son's name was Dane Peters. The rest of the world called him the Rest Stop Dentist.

Not everybody from Dane's many court sessions came that night. The watch room only held thirty chairs, and nine were taken up by the cops who had arrested my son, two local reporters, and Sven Gödel, a freelance journalist from Chicago.

When the guards led my son into the execution chamber, he strode tall, his face bereft of emotion. While one officer unshackled Dane, the other made ready the straps on the cross-like table where Dane would serve his final sentence. Unencumbered, Dane stretched his arms wide, bent back at the waist, and rocked forward to meet my eyes.

A chill ran down my spine. He looked so calm, the exact opposite of me. I could feel my hands shaking around the Bible I clutched to my stomach. *Oh, God, they're actually going to kill my child.* If I had died, they would have called Dane an orphan, but what would they call a childless mother? At fifty-five, I was left all alone.

Dane groped at the front of his orange jumpsuit, patted it flat, and turned toward the awaiting table. Never breaking eye contact, he craned his neck so he could keep a bead on me. My baby boy was in there somewhere, hiding behind that cold stare. I felt myself reaching for him, though I hadn't meant to do so.

Someone tapped me on the shoulder. I turned my head to find a man wearing a police officer's uniform.

"You know," he said, "that's two-way glass. He can't actually see you."

Looking back at my son, I tried to tell myself that the man behind me was wrong. He had to be. Dane was gazing directly at me, *into* me. He sat on the edge of the metal table, twisted, and threw his legs up onto the surface, then lay back and looked toward the ceiling. The guards went about belting him down. Dane lifted his head, met my eyes, and gave me a mirthless smile.

The officer behind me said, "That monster must think he's something. Look at that smug expression painted all over his mug. He ain't a bit sorry 'bout what he done."

Dane blinked twice and settled back on the table.

Too low for anyone else to hear, I said, "He's not a monster. He's my son."

Dane was thirty years old when they put an IV in his arm and dosed him with pentobarbital to render him unconscious. A pump injected him with pancuronium bromide to relax his breathing until his lungs quit altogether. Potassium chloride, the "humane

8

drug," ceased the beating of his heart before the failure of his lungs became too painful. I watched, seated with the families of the victims, while my son was put down like a rabid dog.

One of the men behind the glass finally said, "It's over."

The father of Lillie Mason clapped, putting his hands together, slowly at first, then faster. Vickie Hancock's mother joined in. Fredericka Devereau's parents followed along until everyone surrounding me fell into a fit of raucous applause. I didn't feel the need to celebrate my child's death, so I remained stoic and silent.

Dane's body was transferred from the execution table to a beige body bag atop the stainless surface of an awaiting gurney. I'd seen enough.

Rising from my chair, I took an unsteady step forward and almost fell. A hand wrapped around my bicep, keeping me upright. Glancing to see who'd saved me from a tumble, I came face to face with that Chicago journalist, Sven Gödel.

He asked, "Are you all right?"

"Leave me alone." I snatched my arm from his grasp, turned on my heel, and headed for the door.

Sven called after me, "We should talk, Mrs. Peters."

I didn't justify his comment with an answer.

The watch room door opened onto a courtyard surrounded on all sides by razor-wire-topped fencing. October in Arkansas wasn't quite as cool as back home in Colorado. In fact, the air was uncomfortably warm, like sitting down on a public toilet and finding the previous user's body heat radiating up into in my own butt. Sweat popped out on my forehead. I swiped it away with the back of one hand.

At the main gate, a bald prison guard let me out into the free world. I thought of it like that, "the free world," because during Dane's trial and the time up until his death, I'd felt like a prisoner alongside him. With Dane gone, I was free.

I crossed the parking lot to my gold Camry. Once behind the wheel, I let my emotions take over. Tears choked me. To clear my pipes, I lit a Virginia Slim and allowed the menthol to soothe my clogged throat.

I smoked the entire cigarette in less than three minutes. I rolled down my window and flicked the butt into the prison's lot, leaving a piece of myself behind. Lighting another one, I drove away from that edifice of justice, wondering what else I had left back there. That thought haunted me across seven hundred miles, two fast-food cheeseburgers, four restroom breaks, and a whole pack of Slims, until I crossed the city limits of Well Being, Colorado. Home sweet home.

I pulled into my driveway on autopilot that Saturday afternoon, much as I'd been during the entire trip. Dane hadn't even been dead twenty-four hours, but it seemed as if months had passed. All of a sudden, time was an odd concept to me. What was I supposed to do now?

I took my luggage from the trunk and dragged it into my dank house. The musty aroma of closed-up home hung thick in the air. I dropped my bags in the hallway and went around opening every window in the place.

Everything appeared filthy, disused, and forgotten. Had I personified my living room, I'd have said the floral-print sofa seemed forlorn and the brown shag carpet lonesome. Even the ceiling fan over the coffee table looked depressed.

A dull headache throbbed at the base of my skull. In the kitchen, I found a bottle of Tylenol. I took three and went to lie down on the couch.

Almost fourteen hours later, I awoke with my Bible between my head and the arm of the sofa.

I needed church in the worst way. I went to take a shower and get ready for the Lord's day. Once dressed in what counted as my Sunday best, I grabbed my Bible and headed out to the car.

I drove four miles to Well Being First Baptist on the outskirts of town. The parking lot bustled with people dressed for church. A group of children, ages ranging from five to ten, played a game of tag in the grassy section to the right of the main building. Their playful shouts were sweet, innocent. I tried not to think about Dane at that age as I walked toward the glass doors of the church. But I still saw my son playing with the other kids, face ruddy with exertion, his laughter screechy and pleasant. My memory of him changed. He became a grown man wearing his orange jumpsuit, grunting and lurching after the squealing children, his countenance drawn into a rictus of black rage. He snatched up one little girl and held the child aloft by her ponytail. When she tried to scream, he stuffed his fist into her mouth. With a grunt, Dane yanked a set of chattering teeth from between the girl's cheeks.

I walked right into Meredith Pearce. She let out a squeak, bringing me back to reality. The Sunday school instructor surveyed me from head to foot. She was a compact woman, rosy in the cheeks, face framed by curly black hair. Her pink dress was impeccable, all sharp creases and clean lines.

"Oh, Ella," Meredith said as if I'd been someone different when she'd first set her eyes on me. Her tone changed as she repeated herself. "*Oh… Ella?*"

I gave her a brief smile. It took everything I had. "Sorry about that."

"About what?"

"Running into you."

She stared at me, confusion darkening her pale face. "You're… why are you here?"

"What?" She'd caught me off guard. I didn't understand her question. I regained my composure and said, "I've been away. I wanted to get back to church."

"Uh… I'm not sure… well, you know."

I searched her eyes for meaning but couldn't settle on any reasoning for her strange behavior. "No. I don't think I *do* know."

"I really didn't expect to see you… *around*. You know, after everything that happened." She leaned in and whispered, "People have been talking."

"About what?"

She looked at me as if I'd just asked her why flowers smelled like pork chops. "Ella… your *son*."

My back stiffened as my pulse ramped up. "You can't be serious."

"I just don't think now is the proper time for—"

"And when would be the proper time? I just lost my son, and you're telling me I'm not welcome at my own church?"

She cringed. "Lower your voice, please." She put a hand on my arm. "I'm looking out for your best interest, Ella. You know how people talk."

I shook off her hand. "Behind my back, I suppose."

"I don't suffer gossip, but some say that you should have known. That a mother *would have* known."

Gritting my teeth, I tried to hold back my anger. I couldn't have cared less about making a scene, but I didn't want to give those shallow-minded imbeciles the benefit of seeing me break down from where they sat up on their high horses. "And you call yourself a Christian. You ought to be ashamed of yourself."

Meredith's entire body went rigid, as if I'd shoved a fence post up her hind end.

"As should you. I think you should leave now."

She stormed away, depriving me of the chance to respond, her pink dress swishing around her pistoning legs. She approached a group of mousy women, pointed in my direction, and began gesticulating wildly. All I heard of the discussion was "Her nerve!" before I headed back to my car.

On the way home, I tried praying for Meredith, but everything came out forced or sarcastic. When I asked God to forgive her, I actually laughed. I needed to calm down before I spoke with Him again or risk suffering His wrath.

My house felt even stuffier than before—thick and humid. I had to do something about the smell. From the cabinet under the kitchen sink, I grabbed a can of Pledge, a duster, and a pair of rubber gloves. I set to work in the living room, spraying and dusting to the point of almost wearing the varnish off the coffee and end tables. Moving to the bookshelves on the wall with the room's sole window, I began pulling fantasy novels and thrillers from their hideaways, top to bottom.

On the second row from the bottom, I tugged on a fistful of Trey Franklin mysteries then stalled. One by one, the books tumbled from my grasp, two of them landing open, cracking the already weathered spines further. I leaned in to get a better look at the out-of-place object the paperbacks had hidden for what must have been over twenty-five years.

Putting one fist to my chest, I brought my other hand to my mouth. From behind my fingers, I whispered, "My God."

I had cleaned those bookshelves every spring since I'd bought them in 1983, the year Dane was born. I was positive the toy hadn't been there five months prior in May.

Prince Adam stared back at me, his plastic body grimy with aged dust. With a shaking hand, I picked up the long-forgotten action figure. I sat down in front of the bookcase and wept over the toy that had been the catalyst to everything going wrong in my life.

TWO

LIKE MOST BOYS GROWING UP in the eighties, Dane had an obsession with everything He-Man related. When he wasn't watching the animated series, my son was playing with his vast collection of Masters of the Universe action figures. By his fourth birthday, he had the entire collection, complete with the Castle Grayskull play set and Prince Adam's tiger-like companion. I knew most of the toys' names by heart because Dane wouldn't shut up about them.

One afternoon, two weeks after Dane turned four, he was playing with his toys in the middle of the living room floor, between the coffee table and the television. I was in the kitchen, organizing bills at the dining table, when I heard the rumbling of an engine out front. Standing up, I glanced out the window above the sink. Phil's truck sat in the driveway. Something went icy in my chest. It was Monday, just after noon, and Phil shouldn't have been home yet.

I heard the thud of my husband slamming the truck door. He lumbered across the grass, shoulders hunched, cheeks puffing with exaggerated breaths. I rushed to the front door.

Dane called, "Mommy, what's wrong?"

Moving into the foyer, I said, "Stay there and play, baby. It's just Daddy."

The front door swung open, barely missing me, and I drew back.

Phil's head snapped up. "They cut my hours."

Without waiting for a response, Phil threw the door closed and shoved past me, heading for the kitchen. I slunk back into the living room, where Dane played, oblivious to his father's enraged entrance.

"Dane?"

He looked up at me and smiled. "Uh huh?"

"I'm going to be in the kitchen talking with Daddy. Just keep playing with your toys, okay?"

"Uh huh," he repeated, going back to the warring action figures grasped in his small hands.

When I stepped into the kitchen, Phil was seated at the dining table, sheaves of paper strewn all about in front of him. He picked through them, grunting and fuming.

Without looking up at me, he asked, "What're we gonna do now, Ella?"

"What happened?"

"They cut my hours in half at the yard's what happened. Said they don't need me full time right now. Can you believe that? All them new trains comin' in over the past few months and they're cuttin' me back? I thought for sure I was lookin' at overtime."

"They cut your hours?"

"That's what I said, woman! You deaf?"

I took no offense to the jibe, letting him have his anger. Phil cussed his own mother, but he didn't mean anything by it. Suddenly, I didn't want to be in my own house anymore. I focused on the bills scattered across the table. I'd been planning on running errands before

Phil made it home that evening, but I hadn't gotten around to it. It seemed like the perfect time to do just that.

"I was just… headed out." My words sounded like a ridiculous excuse, even to me. I added, "To pay the water and electric."

"How we gonna pay this crap? Huh? Your nursing job barely puts gas in your tank." He shook his head. "Nope. We're screwed. I ain't got time to find another job. Ain't no jobs to be had, no way. Damn it!" He hammered the table with the ball of his fist again.

"We'll be all—"

"How? You going to start selling ass after you get off work?"

"Don't be crass. You know I don't like that kind of talk." I sat down next to him at the table and wrapped one of his big hands in both of mine. "We'll work through this. Trust me. Okay?"

Phil's anger melted into sorrow. The shift was quick and unexpected, rather jarring. He pulled his hand out of my grasp. "Thought you had to leave."

"I do, but—"

He waved at me. "Go on, then."

Standing up, I called toward the living room, "Dane, get everything cleaned up. We have to—"

"You can leave 'im here. We'll do… something." Phil shrugged. "Might as well use this time off to get to know my son better, huh?"

I forced a laugh. "Are you sure you're in the mood to watch a four-year-old?"

"He's my kid, too, Ella. I'll manage. Might take my mind off"—he ran a hand over the statements in front of him—"this crap."

Before leaving, I gave them both pecks on their cheeks.

I wasn't gone more than an hour.

When I got back, the front door was locked. I didn't remember having secured the dead bolt before leaving, but I figured I must have. I used my key and stepped inside.

The house was quiet, eerily so. I moved through the foyer and into the living room. The furniture had been rearranged. Phil sat on the couch, which he'd turned sideways, with his foot up on the coffee table. A bag of ice rested on his left ankle. The broom from our cleaning closet lay across his lap.

Dane stood with his back to me, facing the wall beside his father, sobbing. A large circle had been drawn on the wall. Dane's face rested in the middle of it. He had to stand on tiptoes to keep it there. My son shook, his entire body quaking, but his bare calves trembled the worst. Four red, parallel lines marked the back of his legs. One of them bled a thin line of bright red down into his left shoe.

My mind ran circles around itself, trying to figure out what I was seeing.

Dane's legs faltered, and he dropped down an inch so that his heels touched the floor. Quick like a whip, Phil snapped the broom handle. The length of wood smacked Dane's legs, drawing a fresh line in his already ruddy flesh. Dane shot back up to his tiptoes.

"Phil!"

Phil settled an indifferent gaze on me. "What? He almost killed me, Ella. I'm teaching him a lesson."

"What are you talking about?"

"After you left, I come out of the kitchen and damn near snapped my ankle on one them toys o' his. Coulda broke my neck! He just left it out for anybody to trip over. I took it away from him and put it up on the shelf. I gave him what for, and I went back into the kitchen to get some ice. When I come back out again, I'll be damned if he wasn't reachin' up to that bookshelf to get that toy. This ain't his house. He can't just be doing whatever. So I'm teaching him like my daddy taught me."

"He's bleeding!"

"He'll be all right, woman. He's tough."

"Phil, he's four. He doesn't know any better."

"Well, he does now, don't he?" Phil used the broom stick to nudge Dane in the side. "Go on. Let your momma clean you up."

Dane raced from the wall and wrapped his thin arms tightly around my legs. Gently, I pushed him away and knelt in front of him. His pale face was lined with new and old tears. I reached up and wiped them away with my thumbs. His chest hitched as he tried to control his sobs.

Running my fingers through his hair, I whispered, "It's okay, baby."

"I… I'm sorry, Momma. I wuh-wuh-won't leave my t-t-toys out again."

"See?" Phil said from the couch. "Told ya he learned his lesson."

Over Dane's shoulder, I shot an angry glance my husband's way. Phil raised his eyebrows questioningly but didn't say a word.

I stood and led Dane to the hallway. "Go to the bathroom and wait on me, sweetie. Go on."

Dane limped away and disappeared into the washroom.

I turned to Phil. "You went too far. You made him bleed."

"He'll be all right. Calm down."

"Calm down? Calm *down*?"

Phil's gaze traveled down to the broomstick on his lap. "Watch yourself, Ella. I'm not in the mood." He spoke in such a calm tone that my blood froze in my veins. The fact that he didn't look at me only served to scare me further.

"Besides," he continued, "I'll take him to the park or somethin' tomorrow. He'll have some fun, and this'll all be behind us. He won't forget, mind you. He'll never forget the lesson."

Shaking, I said, "I have… I have to go clean him up."

Phil nodded. He still wasn't looking at me. "Don't apologize for what I done, Ella. 'Member that. You do, and you'll undermine everythin' I did here today."

Leaving my husband in the living room, I went to see about Dane. Still, Phil's voice echoed in my mind.

Watch yourself, Ella. I'm not in the mood.

THREE

I HAD TO TAKE OUT A mortgage — the first one since Phil paid off the original lien twenty years prior — so that I could bury Dane. The prison system offered to inter him for three thousand dollars, but I refused. Seven days after his death, Dane's body arrived by air freight at the cost of twelve hundred dollars. I spent that entire week scrubbing my house from top to bottom, washing clean clothes, and organizing already alphabetized bookshelves. What took Dane's body so long getting home, I hadn't a clue. The shipping manifest said the parcel — funny thing to call a plain, pine casket — had been damaged in transit. I checked with the funeral home in Denver, and the director said everything was in order and that the casket looked untouched. One coffin, fit for the son I still loved, cost me nine thousand dollars. Dane was worth the money, no matter what he'd done to deserve his fate. Another thirty-five hundred placed him in the ground next to his father. The tombstone set me back four hundred. Having my son home: priceless.

Phil died of emphysema in 2003, ten years before Dane's execution. Whether my smoking got him or not, I didn't know.

"Ella," he'd say, "you'll be the death of me."

I guessed Phil was right because he never touched a cigarette in all his days, but he'd lived with my smoking for twenty years. I smoked during Phil's eulogy and enjoyed the irony of it all. I never cried for my husband, but I wept for Dane.

Three months after Phil passed away, I saw a news report about a girl's body having been found at a rest stop in Arkansas. The girl's name was Lillie Mason. Dane's first victim might as well have been a celebrity for all the attention she got. Details were thin, but somehow, I knew she was important. I followed the case and made notes when other bodies popped up all over the Midwest. Years went by, three to be exact, and Sven Gödel crawled out from under his rock. Sven coined the term the Rest Stop Dentist in an article for the *Chicago Tribune*. Dane had reached twelve kills by then. My baby boy was a busy little guy.

Warnings were posted at rest areas from Kansas to Vermont, even though Dane never went as far north as New England. Some gave advice on how to survey surroundings for possible threats, while others came right out and admonished that the state was not responsible for a citizen's wellbeing. That last one came after Lillie Mason's father—the one who began the applause at Dane's execution—tried to sue the entire state of Arkansas in a civil wrongful death case. The case never went before a judge. The state settled out of court.

A representative for the state of Arkansas went on record saying, "From here on out, all of our rest stops will be manned by security personnel."

Fat lot of good that did. Dane killed another five people at Arkansas rest stops over the course of his career. No more wrongful death cases arose, though. In the end, I figured Lillie Mason's father had simply been money hungry.

Years later, no one would be caught dead at my son's funeral—aside from Dane, of course, and only because he had no say in the matter—so I mourned in solitude.

The mortuary hired a preacher to read from the Bible. "In the sweat of thy face shalt thou eat bread, till thou return unto the ground; for out of it wast thou taken: for dust thou art, and unto dust shalt thou return." Afterward, the preacher gave me a perfunctory nod, then a curt, "Have a nice day," and left without another word.

I stayed until the groundskeeper filled in the hole, covering my son under six feet of earth. Dirty men with shovels had interred Phil. Dane got a backhoe. The sweaty man behind the wheel kept staring at me. He might have been thinking I was crazy for hanging around so long, but probably not. He knew who I was. I was Ella May Peters, the mother of the Rest Stop Dentist.

The afternoon of Dane's funeral, I left the cemetery with plans of doing some much needed shopping. During my wait for his body to be shipped home, I had survived on pizza and Chinese food, all delivered. Old Mother Hubbard's cupboards were bare, and I had grown tired of Italian pies and fried noodles.

When I pulled in, the Fresh Market's parking lot was nearly empty. A uniformed employee stood at the side of the brick-faced building, smoking a cig and talking on a cell phone. I nodded at him as I got out of the car, but he ignored me. He couldn't have been more than twenty, with a face riddled with acne. His hair shone a startling bleach-blond, making it look almost platinum in the glow of the building's perimeter lights.

The automated doors slid open as I approached the storefront. A bin of cantaloupes and a crate of zucchini were on sale directly inside and to my left. From beside the specially-priced items, I grabbed a basket, doubting I would need an entire shopping cart.

Yanni, or some other such New Age nonsense, floated on the air, just loud enough to hear yet soft enough not to grate on my nerves. I perused the fresh produce, squeezing fruit and knocking on melons, smelling stems and hunting spots of decomposition. I picked up a couple of cucumbers, some kale for a salad, and two avocados I planned to have for breakfast.

Routine settled me. If I thought about Dane, or my past in general, I'd wind up crouched in a corner, worshipping Kleenex like Gollum coveting the One Ring. Lord of the Rings analogies aside, I was shopping to replace something I'd lost. With the goods I purchased, I was also buying a section of time—another moment spent not thinking about Dane.

At the back of the store, two women stood beside the fish counter, whispering between themselves. I didn't know either lady, but they seemed to recognize me. With Sven Gödel's articles and his upcoming book venture, my face was well-known to locals and non-locals alike. The woman on the left, a redhead with a bottom bigger than her top, caught me looking and immediately turned back to her crimson-faced friend, who had more lumps and bumps than I cared to count. The ginger and her hefty friend put their backs to me, pretending to eye the catch of the day.

Still, I could hear them snickering. I wanted to ask what the hell was so funny but refrained. The last thing

I needed was to make a scene and have myself labeled as crazy as my wayward son.

In my peripheral vision, a flash of orange caught my eye. The blur disappeared behind a row of condiments and salad dressing about thirty feet across the store from me. Startled, I clutched my chest with the hand not holding my basket of produce. I wasn't sure why I had such a reaction to the orange blur. Surely, it was just another customer. But something didn't feel right.

My heart banged away as I rounded a flat of lemons and limes, headed toward where I'd seen the orange anomaly. I passed the bank of cash registers.

A teenaged clerk grinned from behind a register, her braces catching the soft lights and glittering. "Finding everything okay?"

I nodded. Under the New Age music, a rough humming rose, like someone with a chest cold trying to find the melody of a tune. Though the rhythm was off, I knew the song. Not knowing why, I started to sing along. "Amazing grace, how sweet the sound…" I trailed off when I realized the humming had stopped.

I turned into the aisle where I'd seen the blur disappear. Dried pastas to my right and organic coffee to my left, but I spotted no sign of the orange-clad person. I walked farther and made it to the midpoint of the rows of shelving when I heard that cold-addled throat humming again. The sound seemed to come from everywhere, passing through me like a specter through a wall. The sensation caused me to turn around much quicker than I intended. I almost lost my balance but maintained my stance by bracing a hand on a shelf filled with jars of spaghetti sauce. The bottles tinkled together as I shoved them back on the shelf.

Softly, I said, "Hello?"

I could have cut the quiet with a rubber mallet. Even the New Age soundtrack was gone from the scene, silenced. I took a tentative step forward, then another. I held my produce out in front of me as if I were Van Helsing with a cross of cucumbers come to slay Dracula with my holy avocados. If only I'd had the foresight to grab a head of garlic.

I prayed for some kind of noise. It didn't matter what. I would have given all of Solomon's gold, and a great many of his wives, to hear someone clear their throat or pass gas. I wasn't picky. I felt utterly alone, as if the rapture had come and my Lord had forgotten about little old me.

Louder, I repeated, "Hello?"

A voice thundered, that of a man at the height of his anger. "Get back here, you little bastard!"

Time stood still, as did I. My husband's words echoed through my mind. Someone had pressed Rewind on my life, and I was reliving a terrible memory. My progression halted, I stared toward the end of the shelving where the end-caps would be, expecting at any moment to see my dead husband dragging our son across the gap by the back of his shirt.

Phil's voice echoed and died away. Though the store's music system had not returned, I could hear a newer, subtler sound — the soft whimpering of a child.

I moved down the aisle, quickening my pace as I went. When I reached the end, I looked right, then left, finally settling on a small form propped up against the end-cap.

Given his size, the boy was no more than seven. He was curled into a fetal position, sobbing, his hands covering his face. He slid his hands away slowly, and I gasped.

Dane looked up at me with dark, wet eyes, his brown hair a mess. The He-Man T-shirt he wore was stained with tears. "Wh-why? Why did-didn't you d-d-do anything?"

I moved away from him, backing into the aisle. Laughter came from behind me.

Spinning around, I searched for the source. At the opposite end of the aisle, I saw another flash of orange. The image remained just long enough for me to tell it was a good-sized man clothed in orange from head to foot. The figure vanished behind the corner.

I was done. I'd seen enough, even if I didn't understand what I was seeing. If I didn't get my pulse under control, I'd die of a heart attack in the Italian food section of the Fresh Market. Not a classy way to go, I imagined.

Someone grabbed my shoulder. I whipped around, my arm carrying the basket outstretched, meaning to bash the brains out of whoever had grabbed me.

The cashier with the mouth of metal squealed and leapt back just in time to dodge my assault. I was so startled that I released the basket in mid-swing. The plastic crate flew into a row of shelving. Boxes of dried pasta spilled out onto the floor around me and the scared teenager.

"I heard you calling for help. I'm… I'm sorry I scared you." Her eyes were as wide as grapefruits.

My hands shook as I brought them to my face. I wiped cold sweat from my brow.

"No, no, it's all right. My fault. Let me clean this up."

"I'll get it, lady." The young man from outside must have finished with his smoke break. He walked into the aisle, stooped, and began replacing the fallen boxes of pasta.

I scooped up my basket, picked up whatever produce had spilled out, and followed the cashier back to the front of the store. I had more shopping to do, but I refused to do it there.

As she rang up my items, I asked, "What's wrong with your music system?"

"It does that every night at this time. We stay open an hour longer than we used to, but the music system was never reprogrammed."

I paid my total and left the store. My groceries in the trunk and myself back behind the wheel, I delayed in starting the car. My hands still shook. I wrapped them around the steering wheel, white-knuckle tight, and prayed. "Please, Lord, see me through this. Your grace and wisdom are infinite, whereas I am lost. Shepherd me in my time of need."

Those words usually calmed me, but not that day. I kept hearing Dane's voice asking me why I hadn't done anything.

Sitting in that parking lot, I reflected on my reasoning.

I never hated Phil, for the same reason I held no ill will toward Dane. Phil was my husband, and I was due him my companionship, in good times and bad, or so my vows said. The Bible told about the laws governing marriage. It was a lifelong commitment. Who was I to go against the word of God?

Dane was of me, my child, a part of my eternal existence. His crimes meant nothing as far as my heart was concerned. My mind considered his murders abhorrent, evil, but there would be no swaying my internal feelings for him. I had failed Dane enough. I owed him my undying love, just as I owed Phil my presence.

God had a funny way when it came to dealings with me. He'd grant me small victories then punish me lightly with financial burdens so that I wouldn't forget that I needed to rely solely on Him. I was reminded constantly of that picture showcasing a beach with a single set of footprints in the sand. The caption, no matter the artist, always read the same, something to the effect of, "During the worst times, Jesus carried me." I could see myself as a burden on the Lord, as I could see my life as my own cross to bear.

But in the end, it all came back to a family life I couldn't have, mistakes I might have skirted given a little strength and a whole bunch of faith. God forgives all, so the Bible said.

Ten years of my life had been filled to the brim with loneliness. Phil was dead, and Dane was out killing people while I sat at home and dug my heels into Christianity. Filled to the brim with my savior, I became a child of God. Cleaning, reading, and existing became my way. Those years seemed to pass in a blur of gray, indistinguishable and cloudy. I didn't like to think about them.

Then they caught Dane, and I once again had a purpose to my life. For over three years, I traveled, chasing down a man who had once been my baby boy, my Dane. When I finally found what had become of him, I felt that black hole in my heart cave in further, the perimeter grew wider, and at some point, I fell into it. I'd found my own personal hell. Even in the midst of God and His angels, I lamented in flames.

I supposed I deserved my suffering. Self-imposed ridicule was something I dealt with by not dealing with it. After all, when I died, I would be going to heaven. So all I had to do was wait.

Amazing grace, how sweet the sound, that saved a wretch like me.

FOUR

LILLIE MASON WAS MY SON'S first victim. I learned a bit about her during Dane's trial. Lillie had been blond with a thin build. Her smile wasn't a pretty one and always seemed forced, no matter what picture they passed around the courtroom. She didn't look like a happy girl. Maybe that was why Dane homed in on her that night in Arkansas. In Dane's testimony, he admitted to lurking in the ladies' restroom.

His exact words were, "I perv'd her out from over the top of one of the stall doors. I'm surprised she didn't see me. I was doing a piss-poor gopher impression."

She drove a red Dodge Neon that authorities found parked at the rest stop between Mile Marker 23 and the turnoff to Homesboro. The engine was still running. Walter Bingham, a part-time state trooper, had seen Lillie's car two hours earlier when he'd pulled through to check for campers and squatters.

At the trial, Trooper Bingham stated, "When I come back 'round, I seen that same red Neon, parking lights still on, no one inside, so I stopped to check it out. I began my search in the ladies' room, making myself known before entering."

The prosecutor, Kent Parker, Esq., asked, "And what time was this, Officer Bingham?"

"Two a.m. on the dot. Since I was sure something was wrong, I made note of the time before leaving my cruiser."

"Thank you," Parker said. "Please continue."

"I entered the ladies' room after making myself known, like I said. I checked each stall, then went one step further and looked inside the men's room, just to make sure. No one was there. I called it in to headquarters and had 'em run the license plate. When it came back with Lillie Mason's face on my computer, I felt this stinging sensation in my gut. I knew what'd happened to her right then and—"

"Please, Officer Bingham, stick to the facts."

"Okay. I waited for backup to arrive. When Roger Nutmeager showed up, me 'n' him did a sweep of the perimeter. We found Lillie Mason's body without much difficulty. The state has these big ol' trash receptacles that pack themselves. All the rest areas have got 'em. Sorry, I don't know the right word for 'em. Anyway, Lillie was 'round back o' the restrooms, in the trash compactor. She'd been smashed. She looked like a steam roller'd been over her." Officer Bingham turned greener than a leprechaun's coat and tails. He put a fist to his mouth, and his Adam's apple bobbed.

Gasps erupted from the audience, and I felt sick, as well, but I had a weight upon me. I couldn't have gotten up if I tried, much less have found the strength to walk away.

"I'm sorry you had to see that," Parker said, "but you said you found her 'without much difficulty.' Please, tell us how you came about finding her in the compactor, Officer Bingham. This part is very important."

"Sorry, buddy, I don't like thinking about it, but here goes. Roger's the one who seen 'em first. There's this concrete walkway that goes 'round the building that houses the toilets. Like a wrap-a-round sidewalk, I reckon. We'd only made it to the corner of the women's restroom when Roger puts his hand on my chest and tells me to hold on. We didn't need our flashlights. The lights from the building were plenty. Someone had laid out a trail of bloody teeth, one right after another, maybe two feet apart. I kept thinking about that kid's story, you know... Hansel and Grendal."

Parker said, "For the record, it's Hansel and *Gretel*, but go on, Officer Bingham."

"Yeah. Gretel." Bingham's eyes drifted. He seemed lost in memory. I didn't envy him. "Only, Lillie Mason didn't make it to grandmother's house. Instead, that sicko" — Bingham nodded at Dane, who sat still and quiet in his neatly pressed orange jumpsuit — "ripped out all of her teeth and threw her away."

FIVE

THE FIRST PERSON TO VISIT me after Dane's burial was Talia Stemsford. Talia had run the library in Well Being, Colorado—where I'd lived my entire life—since the previous head librarian had died of a stroke in '99. She was a polite, book-smart lady, five-foot nothing, with long chestnut hair that hung to her backside. She wore it in a ponytail more often than not. Talia worshipped Jehovah and abhorred crosses with Jesus upon them. Sacrilege, her faith called it. So when she showed up at my door, I knew she meant well, as every wall in my home had a crucifix upon it—some bearing my savior and others not. But I still figured our conversation would be awkward.

Talia knocked on my door just after I'd finished lunch that day, her rapping reminding me of a headache I'd been ignoring. In the two weeks since Dane's funeral, I hadn't been sleeping well. I decided to answer the knock before taking some Tylenol with a sherry chaser. I opened the door with a Virginia Slim pinched in my teeth.

Running her hand down her front, Talia straightened her red cardigan. Her hands went to her sides, where she began fidgeting with her ankle-length jean skirt. She looked so meek, I almost laughed. I blew smoke into her face and she waved it away, smiling. "Can I come in, Ella?"

"You witnessing or visiting?"

"Visiting, of course. I wouldn't think of imposing on you, knowing how you feel about my... religion, and after a crisis such as yours."

"Come on in, then."

She held her breath and stepped through my fog of menthol. Standing in the foyer, she gazed into my living room, seemingly eyeing my flower print sofa and Phil's old, worn-down recliner. A pile of sodden tissues sat on the coffee table in front of the couch, remnants of my mourning. Golden sunlight poured through the window on the far wall, and swirling dust motes waltzed to an unheard melody.

I led Talia to the left, into the kitchen, where I pointed at one of the dining table chairs. She pulled it out and sat down.

"Your house smells delicious. Is that cinnamon?"

"Glade Plug-ins. Vanilla-scented, I think. You're probably just smelling the freshener mixing with the smoke." I stamped out my cigarette in an ashtray that sat dead center on the kitchen table.

Talia gave me a small smile and slid the ceramic bowl full of butts farther from her. "This place is spotless. Tell me, how *do* you keep up with it?"

"A little elbow grease and boredom go a long way."

"Grief, too, I would suppose."

Wanting to change the subject, I said, "Coffee?"

Talia stood, swept her skirt up under her, and sat back down. "Black, please, and thank you."

I was reaching for the cabinet door above the stove when she said that. I stopped, posed like some

Renaissance statue, remembering how Dane used to say that same thing.

My mind skipped into the past, to an afternoon long forgotten. "Would you like a peanut butter and jelly sandwich, Dane?"

He smiled, missing one tooth or another, and said, "Please and thank you, Momma." That was before he killed people.

Across the kitchen, Talia gave me an odd look. Reality seemed broken, past and present blending together. Dane stood in the middle of the kitchen, his goofy, toothless smile summoning me to act.

My pulse escalated at the sight of my child. A dull thud sounded in my ears. Dane was out of place, unmarred by time, seven years old again. I knew I was seeing a memory, but other thoughts invaded, making him seem all too real. I needed to make that sandwich for him—crunchy peanut butter and grape jelly slathered on Iron Kids white bread and a glass of milk with a bendable straw peeking from the lip of the glass. Dane would eat while I hummed the tune of "That Old Rugged Cross" or "Amazing Grace."

Dane spilled his milk, that clumsy little boy, and Phil came in all thunder and presence, like Zeus himself, and beat the boy until Dane's ears bled. It was only milk. We could buy more. I could hear myself saying it, but not acting upon that motherly urge to protect my child. Phil stormed away, growling and cussing, and I knelt to soothe my battered baby.

Talia said, "Ella? You okay?"

"Yeah." Suddenly out of breath, I managed to add, "Sorry about that. This headache is killing me."

I took the can of Folgers down from the cabinet and put it on the counter. Without starting the maker, I opened the adjacent door and pulled down my extra bottle of Tylenol. The headache was fading, but I wanted to put up a wall should it try to invade once more. I popped three of them, fifteen hundred milligrams of Headache Go Buh-Bye, dry swallowing without thinking. I'd never done that before. I didn't even blink, much less gag.

At the sink, I put water in the carafe, filling it to the ten-cup mark. When I turned around to walk back to the Brewmaster, Dane was standing between me and the coffee maker. He was seven again.

He held out his hand. In the palm was a pink tooth swimming in a sea of blood.

"Will the tooth fairy come even though it didn't fall out on its own, Momma? Will the tooth fairy be mad 'cause Daddy knocked it out?"

Seven-year-old Dane grew into thirty-year-old Dane in an instant. He wore his bright orange prison jumpsuit with ASP901465 above his right breast. He smiled at me, and different teeth were missing. One hand grabbed his other, and Dane cracked his knuckles. "I took their teeth, Momma. Just like Daddy took mine. I'm the tooth fairy, but I don't leave no money."

I screamed. The carafe shattered all over the floor. Shaking uncontrollably, I stared at one piece in particular as it twirled lazily in a puddle of water.

"Oh! Are you all right, Ella?" Talia rose from her chair so fast she knocked it over. "Here, sit down. Lemme clean that up for you. Oh, what you must be going through. Dear, dear, deary. You poor dear."

Talia made quick work of the mess I'd made, only stopping to ask where I kept the broom, dustpan, and mop. She swept up the glass and dumped the wet shards into the trashcan by the fridge. She hummed

"Amazing Grace" softly while she mopped up the water.

I couldn't have cared less about why a Jehovah's Witness was singing a Christian hymn. I was too shaken up. Focusing on the present, trying to rid my mind of the imaginings that had been recently thrust upon me, I prayed and asked God to deliver me from my hallucinations.

With as many things as I'd had broken and destroyed in my lifetime, I kept extras of everything. I told Talia where the backup carafe was, and she pulled it down from the top of the pantry. She made coffee in silence, her humming done for the day. She fixed me a cup, then one for herself, and sat down across from me.

She blew steam from the top of her mug. "You're worse off for wear than I thought you were."

"I'll make it. Been through worse spells than this one."

She looked shocked. "You have?"

"I was talking about dropping the pot, not my son."

"Oh." Talia sipped at her coffee, giving that hot-java-drinker's cringe every time the scalding fluid touched her lips. It never ceased to amaze me at how shocked people were that their coffee was hot.

"So to what do I owe this visit, Talia?"

"If you don't want to talk, I can understand."

"We're having coffee, aren't we? Shoot." I worked on cooling my own coffee with long, belabored exhalations.

"I'm doing a fundraiser at the library. I was wondering if you wanted to get out of the house? You know, come on down and take your mind off things for a while?"

I smiled. "No one else will help out, huh?"

"Not a single soul."

"I suppose I can. You're right." In the reflection on the microwave door across the kitchen, Dane stood behind me with his hands on my shoulders, though I couldn't feel them. My grip on the hot mug tightened. I closed my eyes and willed Dane away. When I opened them, my son was gone.

I told Talia, "I definitely need to get out of this house."

###

After Talia left, I saw no more of my dearly departed son that day. Thank God for that, as I don't think I could have handled more hallucinations. I did the dishes in silence, a perfunctory measure to keep my mind off things. I washed Talia's cup four times and scrubbed my mug so hard I might have worked off some of the gloss. I put the two cups and the carafe in the drainer and went to lie down on my bed.

The quiet was menacing. I swore I could hear demons and imps chattering in darkened corners. I crawled atop my comforter without pulling it away and rolled over onto my back. The ceiling fan spun languidly above me. I desperately needed to clean the blades. I felt my eyes following the revolutions of the fan, and the blades seemed to slow, an optical illusion Dane used to enjoy when he was a kid. While Phil was away at work, Dane would come in and lie down with me during my afternoon naps. I worked evenings at the hospital on the edge of town so I could homeschool Dane. His in-house teachings were a necessity brought on by the bruises Phil left on him. Excuses never made were lies never told, I always said.

Dane and I would both feign sleep on those afternoons, peeking through the slits of our eyes, enjoying our time away from his father. No one ever asked me why I remained with my husband after all the violence, because nobody ever knew what kind of man Phil Peters really was. If they'd asked, though, I would have told them what every beaten woman had said since God uttered, "Let there be light." I stayed for the good times, those brief moments of tenderness Phil would tease me with, hoping that one day he'd see the error of his ways and revert back to the decent man I'd fallen in love with. I would tend to Dane when Phil was done with him, but I never lifted a hand to stop the violence in the first place. I had no idea what I was doing to Dane, as I'm sure Phil couldn't imagine the monster he was creating.

I stared at the ceiling fan and prayed. I asked God to forgive Dane's transgressions and my lack of action while he was growing up. I kept telling myself that there was nothing I could have done. That thought helped me sleep, though I didn't deserve rest or forgiveness.

SIX

DANE PLED GUILTY TO ALL forty-two counts of first-degree murder. He knew there would be no out for him. DNA evidence would have buried him in an avalanche.

I tried to visit him three times when he was at Arkansas State, but he refused my requests. Three months before his execution, he wrote me a letter.

Dear Momma,

My time's over. No need for you to see me anymore.

Dane

I didn't bother running through the million questions I had bouncing around in my skull. I knew I'd see him at the execution.

I supposed him not wanting to see me could have been for any number of reasons, but I doubted that he felt bad for what he'd done.

The first three years Dane was incarcerated, he was shipped from penitentiary to penitentiary. His forty-two crimes stretched over nine different states. Because of that, he had to be tried and found guilty in each state. The process was long and drawn out, but in the end, Arkansas won the right to kill him. Dane took his sentencing in silence. In the courtroom, I was the only one who cried over Dane. His confession of guilt and refusal to appeal expedited his death. Dane spent only nine months inside the walls of Arkansas State Penitentiary before his date with lethal injection.

My, how time flew during that period of my life. I withdrew and used all my savings, which consisted mostly of Phil's death benefits from the railroad, to make sure I was there for all of Dane's court appearances. The only other person besides me to attend every trial was that Chicago journalist, Sven Gödel. Sven stood to make a bucket-load of money where my son was concerned. The ink on his book deal was already dry by the time I buried my son.

Sven reminded me of an ambulance-chasing lawyer, sniffing out the spin to a tragedy that would put his name in lights. I despised the man for that. I didn't wish him poverty, as that wouldn't have been Christian of me, but I reviled the way he used tragedy to garner a leg up in life.

SEVEN

THE EVENING AFTER TALIA STEMSFORD'S request that I help with her fundraiser, Sven phoned. I almost didn't answer the call. I stood in my kitchen, staring at the cordless sitting on its base as if it were some alien thing that would shock me if I risked touching it. I read the caller ID, made a mental note that the only person in Chicago I knew was that low-life journalist, and complained inwardly about my poor luck. I really needed to change my phone number.

I picked up the handset, pressed Talk, and put it to my ear. I didn't say hello. I owed the man no greeting.

A moment of awkward silence hung in the air, a heavy thing that quickened my heart.

He finally said, "Hello?"

"What do you want?"

He cleared his throat. "I've been trying to reach you for a few days. I'm glad you finally answered."

I glanced at the message tally on the phone's base. Four missed calls. I hadn't heard the phone ring once in over a week. "I've been busy. Still am, in fact. What's this about? I have nothing more to say about my son."

"This *is* about Dane, but I don't have any questions. I believe we should meet. I need to show you something."

I told myself that whatever that vulture had to deliver, I wasn't interested. I could hear my breathing echoed in the phone, as I was sure Sven could, also. I sounded like a bull fit to charge. Finally, I said, "What is it?"

"Dane allowed me to interview him before his death. I can't use the footage. No one will buy it. Hard to sell a sympathetic killer, Mrs. Peters."

Sympathetic? I couldn't think of a single bit of information that would make anyone sympathize with Dane. Sven had my attention, and I hated him for it, as well as myself for taking the bait he'd cast. "Video?"

"Yes. Arkansas State recommended I destroy the footage, said no self-respecting publication would purchase it. Wow, were they right! I figured, instead of trashing my hard work, I'd see if you would like to try and get something out of it. His statement is… emotionally charged."

I sighed. I wasn't sure if I had the heart to see my son alive again, but I asked, "When can you come? I'm assuming you're coming to me because I wouldn't be caught dead in your windy city, Mr. Gödel."

"I'll come to you, yes. When is good? I'm in Kansas City today, working on a piece, then I'm free the rest of the week."

I checked the wall calendar: Monday. Talia had written in her fundraising soiree on a Sunday two weeks away. I didn't remember her doing that. "Whenever. Just make it soon. I don't want to be sitting around the house until kingdom come wondering what it is you have to show me."

"Then expect me tomorrow. I'll drive out tonight. Where would you like to meet me?"

"Do you know where I live?"

"Yes, I do."

"Good. Then you'll find me, no problem. Goodbye, Mr. Gödel."

Upon hanging up, I wanted to explode. Grief and uncertainty mixed with my abhorrence for Sven Gödel. Instead of breaking every dish in my kitchen, I fixed a snack of cheese and Tylenol.

Just after dark, I went out to check the mail. I was on autopilot, just going through the motions. At the road, I popped open the mailbox and rummaged inside. Pulling out two envelopes that looked like bills, I paused when I noticed the third item clutched in my hand.

I stuffed the bills in the pocket of my jeans and focused on the folded-up newspaper article that had been secreted away under the rest of my mail. Under the glow of the streetlamps, I pulled open the gray sheet and began to read.

The article was titled "A Mother's Ignorance." The overlong piece written by Sven Gödel went into great detail about Dane's murders and him being caught. Then the subject shifted to me: my trek across the country, following Dane from trial to trial, finally ending at Dane's execution. The journalist called the post-execution applause of the victims' families "a cacophony of justice."

Standing at the edge of my yard, I shook like a detoxing alcoholic. Anger was at the forefront of my mind, but nestled in a deeper drawer of my psyche was an uncanny fear. The more I thought about the *presence* of the article in my mailbox and not the *content* of it, the more my mind reeled. The paper was a snippet, not an entire newspaper. Even so, I didn't subscribe to any periodical and especially not the *Chicago Tribune*. No.

Someone had left that article for me. My rage dissipated completely, and I was left cold and scared at the curb in front of my house.

Still trembling, I went back inside. I needed some rest and time to think. I lay on my bed, watching the ceiling fan again, no longer focused on the dust-bunnies that had collected, mated, and bred above my head. Earlier that day, I'd cracked the window about an inch. Cool fall air drifted in through the slit. From my bed, I could see the stars in my heaven. As with almost everything in the house, the windowpane was spotless. Windex and Mr. Clean had become drugs of sorts, things to use for escape. I needed everything in order or else my head would cave in from the sheer pressure of a banal life.

I held no false conceptions concerning where Dane and Phil had ended up when they left my world. Christianity told plainly about the suffering they would be forced to endure. Forever and ever, amen. I looked to the heavens that night not because I hoped they were up there somewhere, but because I had nowhere else to turn. I pulled the Bible from the drawer of my nightstand and clutched it to my breast. Whatever existence I was to have until the day the Lord deemed fit to usher me home, I would take it with a grain of salt. I couldn't wait to be done with mortal nonsense. I wasn't content with living out my days, months, or years as a human only *being*.

So why had I accepted Talia's request to help with the fundraiser? I surmised that decision was based on nothing more than a will to do something for another person. I didn't expect to redeem myself where Dane was concerned. I wanted to be outside of my house, gone from the constant reminders of the failures in my past, present, and—I assumed—future. Once someone became content with life and how utterly unpredictable and cruel it always turned out to be, they stopped caring and started expecting the worst. Yes, I was sure bad things were waiting for me somewhere over the rainbow.

The window whispered, "Psst."

I bolted upright in the bed.

The noise came again. *"Psst."* The window demanded my attention. The second time, it was longer, more insistent. Almost pleading.

"Get it done!" the voice hissed.

Again, "Psst."

There came a clacking sound, like the pendulum balls of a perpetual motion novelty knocking together, and I shuddered. The noise was vaguely familiar.

When the smacking stopped, the window again whispered, "Psst."

I croaked, "Hello?"

The window fell silent.

Jumping out of bed, I ran the five feet to the window and slammed it shut. I stayed there for some time, breathing rapidly and trying to calm my drumming heart. My hallucinations had returned, but I refused to lend them any credence. I didn't know when I had begun, but I realized I was singing "Amazing Grace." Not the entire tune. Only the first few lines. "Amazing grace… how sweet… the sound…"

I'd dropped the Bible when I got out of bed. I bent over and grabbed it from the floor. "That saved a wretch…"

Something ran past the window. I didn't scream. I only sang louder. I couldn't help myself. It was as if I didn't have control over my own vocal chords. A pressure built in my abdomen, something I figured was fear, until I made water in my panties. "... like me!"

I turned on my bedside lamp, which gave off a cone of light that narrowed the farther out it went. A pair of dusty brown work boots stepped into the diffused glow. They were attached to jean-clad legs. Letting my gaze trail up, I saw what appeared to be the Grim Reaper on casual holiday.

His skinless jaw was slack, opened so I could see the fat tongue behind his teeth. The eyes hid in shadows below a hood. His head tilted quizzically then shook side to side, as if he were disappointed in me. Slowly, Death raised an arm, extended its skeletal hand, and flipped me the bird.

A second person ran between Death and me, too quickly for me to catch a glimpse of his or her face. I squealed and pedaled back a few steps until the backs of my thighs were flush with the mattress.

Laughter erupted, and Death bolted from sight. I stood there, damp between my thighs, wondering what on earth I'd just seen. When I came to my senses, I snatched a pair of clean panties and a fresh pair of jeans from my dresser. I rushed to the kitchen and called the police.

I didn't want to go back into my master bath, so I changed in the guest bathroom in the hallway across from Dane's room. I didn't even consider taking a shower. No way was I going to be caught naked inside my home while crazy people were outside plotting my demise. I locked the door to the bathroom and remained there until I heard the first knock on my door.

I stayed inside while the initial responding officer surveyed the premises. I walked through the house, following the cop, window by window, until he came back around and knocked on the front door.

He was a young guy with a military crew cut. His cheeks glowed, they were so red. He had a gold wedding band on his ring finger. "Is the house secure? No one came inside, right?" His voice was much deeper than I expected, a silky baritone. Barry White had been reincarnated as a white man with rosacea.

"No."

"Recognize these?" He held up a bandana in one hand. The cloth had a skeletal jaw-line painted on the fabric, but I remembered that tongue most of all. In his other hand was a pair of gloves with pale-white metacarpal bones etched on the fingers.

I'd been had. "Yes, I do. That's what they were wearing."

"They?" He looked even younger when he was confused, contrasting his deep voice further.

"Someone ran by just before the guy... or girl wearing those things stepped into the light of my window, then again just before they left me alone. I'm sure there was more than one."

Over the officer's shoulder, I saw another police car arrive. The lights on its roof turned my neighborhood into an azure watercolor painting. A stout man, barrel-chested and bearded, climbed out of the car and approached, adjusting his utility belt as he walked.

"Ma'am." He nodded at me. "I'm Officer Sherwood." His attention shifted to the second policeman. "Whatcha got, Driver?"

"Not much. She says she saw possibly two persons, one wearing these" — Driver held up the items for the new officer to see — "and one that ran by her window twice. They dropped some art on the side of her house, too, looks like."

My stomach churned. "What? They did *what* to the side of my house?"

Officer Driver turned back to meet my eyes. "Sorry about that. Come with me. I'll show you."

He led me down off the front porch and around to the left side of my house. The light from my bedside lamp still made that cone of illumination, and for a minute, I thought I saw those dusty, brown work boots again. Driver played his flashlight over the vinyl siding, and I read the words like someone following a bouncing ball.

Spray-painted in black three-foot-tall letters, from the front of my house to the rear, was the sentence: THEY SHOULD KILL U 2.

Sherwood said, "Well, that's... interesting. Ma'am, do you—"

"Can... can we talk inside? I don't feel safe out here." Without waiting for his response, I walked back around to the front of the house.

When we got back inside, I led the two officers into my kitchen. Sherwood took down my statement at the dining table while Driver searched the interior of the house as a precautionary measure. I offered Sherwood coffee, even though I didn't want to touch my Brewmaster, and he declined. I was fishing for a reason to keep them there longer, as I didn't like the idea of being alone. The officer probably realized that.

Driver came back into the kitchen and nodded at Sherwood. I guessed that meant my home was all clear.

Sherwood had me sign the report, then he stuck his pen in his breast pocket, directly over his badge. "I'll be on the rest of the night. I'll do a couple of drive-bys during my shift, but you probably won't see these kids again."

I looked at him in surprise. "You think they were kids? I told you they were the size of grown men."

"Have you seen the teenage boys around town? I keep telling my wife there's something in the water." Sherwood chuckled.

I latched onto him with a stare that expressed my disapproval of his humor. His chuckle turned into a clearing of the throat.

I asked, "What about the message on my wall? Seems rather *adult* to me."

"Parents are more than likely talking all about your son's crimes, Mrs. Peters. Kids hear these things, and you become the target of teens with nothing better to do. Even though what they wrote is disturbing, it's probably nothing more than stupid teenagers playing dumb games. You were a teen once yourself. You know how it goes."

"I never spray-painted a lady's home after she's just lost her son."

My comment made Sherwood and Driver's eyes connect. When Sherwood looked back at me, he repeated, "You *more than likely* will not see them again. If you do, call me." He handed me his card.

Both men left, and I sat at the kitchen table, staring at Sherwood's card. "Thomas Sherwood. Thomas. *Thomas.*"

"A man named Thomas gave me his teeth, Momma," Dane said from beside the sink. "And his tongue."

I remained calm. I'd had about enough of all the faux-reality playing with my mind. If I was going to be insane, I would go crazy on my own terms. Stoically, I said, "Go away, Dane."

"Doc Morrow says the teeth might lead me home."

I was talking to a loop in my memories, something said in the past. I knew that, but I couldn't recall the time or place. I wondered aloud, "Who was Doc Morrow?"

"Oh, Momma. You'll find out. You'll find out *real* soon."

I ignored Dane for the figment of my imagination that he was and went back to Thomas Sherwood's card, mulling over his name again. Thomas *Flynn* had been one of Dane's victims. A man on a business trip found Flynn hunched over in an unlocked stall at a rest stop in Chickapee, Kansas. Flynn's trail of teeth led to a sink that had been clogged with fistfuls of paper towels. Floating in the stagnant water was Flynn's tongue. The CSI team took many pictures of that seafaring chunk of muscle. Those same photographs were on display at the trial, shown on a flat-screen TV rolled in by a bailiff. Prosecutor Parker made sure each person in attendance saw every high-definition photo. The taste buds on the tongue had swollen and turned white, but the meat underneath had remained a bright, neon pink.

I left that memory behind and got up to leave the kitchen. Fresh underwear and shorts or not, I still hadn't cleaned up after wetting myself. That had been rather low on my priority list. I just hoped Sherwood and Driver hadn't noticed an odor. I might have been a sight embarrassed. I showered in water so hot my entire body was one big welt when I stepped out. I felt clean, though. Alive and refreshed.

When I went back to the kitchen for a dose of Tylenol, Dane was gone… if he'd ever really been there to begin with. I didn't want to look in the sink. I was afraid I'd find Thomas Flynn's tongue.

EIGHT

DANE DROVE A TRUCK FOR East-Western Trailways. The company was based out of Roanoke, Virginia, and had a total of thirteen drivers, Dane included. Dane's rig, a company Peterbilt, had plain white paint with the company logo emblazoned on the doors in bright blues and oranges. I'd only seen the truck in courtroom photographs. Dane's job allowed him the freedom to roam where he pleased as long as he made his delivery dates. Bodies had amassed along my son's route, four per year to be exact. One headline had read: "Rest Stop Dentist's Journey Across Middle America," written by none other than Sven Gödel.

I had never made Dane's housing situation my business, but during his trial, I came to find that investigators assumed he'd been living in the Peterbilt. All his worldly possessions were in there: a paperback copy of *A Christmas Carol*, brand new without a single crease in the binding; a duffel bag that served as a closet of sorts for his clothing; two dirty movies involving Asian women who looked, to my untrained eye, to be grossly underage; a jar of teeth. Dane kept the lower teeth of his victims; he used the upper ones to leave his sick trails. I always imagined he did that because Phil had never knocked out any of his son's bottom teeth.

Dane got used to smiling with his neat line of pearls exposed on the bottom, his upper lip hiding the blank spaces on the top row.

The cab of Dane's Peterbilt was where he'd worked on his victims. Forensic investigators found latent blood residue under the mattress of his bed. Detectives surmised that Dane had removed the mattress before working on his captives. Analysis of the bodies proved the victims had all been alive during the extraction of their teeth, then murdered with a single hatchet blow to the back of the head. In the case of Thomas Flynn, no one guessed at why Dane had removed the man's tongue. But I knew.

Dane had been seven years old the first time he spoke back to his father. I stood in the kitchen, cooking eggs and bacon for breakfast, when I heard Phil call from the living room to Dane in his bedroom. Dane didn't respond, so Phil repeated his request much louder.

Dane's voice came down the hallway, sounding far too aggravated. "Gimme a minute!"

I heard Phil's rise from the couch over the sizzling of bacon in my cast iron; the couch springs sounded that loud. My husband's footsteps echoed off the hardwood floor to the walls of the hallway as he left the carpet of the great room. Dane's door was flung open with so much force that I later discovered the doorknob embedded in the wall.

Dane's screams came next.

I'd been holding an egg. When I looked down, yellow yoke dripped from my palm into a puddle on the floor. A section of jagged shell was stuck deep in my palm; crimson tendrils leaked into the whites and turned pink.

Phil roared, "Keep screaming, and I'ma cut out your tongue!"

So, many years later, while I sat in the courtroom that housed Dane's trial for Thomas Flynn's murder, I heard Phil's voice again yelling his warning of imminent tongue removal, and I figured I was the only one who knew exactly why Flynn's had been removed.

The man hadn't stopped screaming, so Dane had used Phil's words as inspiration.

NINE

THE DAY OF SVEN GÖDEL'S visit, I spent the morning hours on the phone, arguing over what constituted vandalism according to my insurance policy. The lady on the other end kept telling me that the terminology meant a broken window and the like, and since my policy didn't state, in plain English, that graffiti was covered, I would have to pay out of pocket for the painting fees. I asked for her supervisor and was put on hold. Ten minutes later, I finally spoke with someone who had a bit of sense. Mr. Fister assured me I would be compensated for the repairs but that I had to have them completed first. I had the freedom to choose my painter, so that was nice. I thanked him and hung up.

Colin's Walls 'N' Things arrived just after noon. Frank, the man who would be supervising the repainting of my outer wall, was a nice enough fellow until one of his employees whispered in his ear. The whisperer had a name badge sewn into his blue jumpsuit: Stanley. After Stanley spoke his hushed words, Frank's entire countenance changed. Frank and Stanley walked back to their truck without another word. The third painter sat in the truck's cab, staring at me and chewing something that could have been either tobacco or a mound of bubblegum. I never got the third man's name. Frank hollered for the man to get out of the truck, that they had work to do, and he did so. I left them to their job.

My gold Camry sat in the driveway with Frank's truck behind it, so when Sven arrived in his black Mercedes, he had to park on the road in front of my house. I'd been sitting on the porch, drinking lemonade and listening to the painters curse at each other for the past hour. I was glad Sven had shown up when he did. Much longer and I might have said something to Frank and his crew about how one speaks while in the presence of a lady. Whether or not the lady in question was a serial killer's mother was beside the point.

Sven Gödel's platinum-blond hair shone brightly in the afternoon sun, shimmering like a golden pond. His Scandinavian heritage could not be argued, the cheekbones the biggest giveaway, even though he didn't speak with an accent. I made him out to be American-born, but his parents had probably arrived by boat or other conveyance. He wore a three-piece suit, a navy-blue number that made him look awfully businesslike compared to my pink paisley sundress. His tie was loose around his neck, just this side of coming undone. It was the only thing about him that didn't look tight enough to choke a horse.

"Ella," he said, nodding at me while he walked up the cobblestone that cut my yard into two equal parts.

I hitched my chin at him. "Mr. Gödel."

He proffered his hand. "You're looking nice today."

I shook it lightly. "I have my moments." I noted the clear case he held in his right hand.

He held up the plastic sleeve to show me the DVD inside. "Should we start with this, or would you like to speak a little beforehand?"

"What would we say to each other, Mr. Gödel?"

"I'm doing this out of respect for you. I didn't have to come."

"I didn't have to *let* you come, either. So if you've weaseled your way into an attempt at an interview, I'll see that you *leave* quicker than anything. If I'm honest, I don't have an ounce of patience when it comes to you. You should know that up front. So mind your Ps and Qs while you're in my home. Are we understood?"

He leaned in and squinted at me. "Ella, I—"

"I don't want any excuses or tries at winning over my good nature. Any idea of that flew out the window when you wrote that article about how I ignored Dane's doings. What did you call it? 'A Mother's Ignorance'? Yeah, that was it. So you'll come inside, we'll watch your little video, and you will be on your way."

He settled back on his heels. "Fair enough."

"Come on in, then."

As I led Sven inside my home, Frank bellowed at Stanley, calling him an awful homosexual slur.

Stanley replied, "You should know!"

I hoped they would be done soon. I'd had all I could take of their nonsense. I showed Sven into the living room, where he sat on my flower-print love seat. I offered him coffee, and he accepted, so I went into the kitchen and started a pot. While the Brewmaster did its duty, I returned to the living area and used the proper remotes to turn on the fifty-inch TV Phil had bought just before he died choking on the fluid in his lungs. I powered up the DVD player, and the tray slid open. Sven handed me the disc, and I slipped it into the tray. I pushed it closed. The disc auto-started, so I pressed Pause on the remote.

On the screen, Dane sat in a tan room, across the table from the camera. Sven was nowhere in sight, so I assumed he was seated behind the recording device. Dane was smiling that same unnerving grin he'd given me during his sentencing. That still-video image broke my heart. I went back into the kitchen to wait for the coffee to finish so Sven wouldn't see me crying.

After the last drip from the coffee maker, I filled two mugs and brought them back into the living room. Sven took his and immediately began sipping at the brew. I guessed he didn't need cream or sugar, so I made no offer. I sat down in Phil's old recliner but didn't lean back. I perched on the edge, like a bird on a wire. Hesitantly, I pressed Play on the remote.

Sven's voice was familiar. "Hello, Dane."

Dane nodded at the camera. His unshaven face settled, and his smile bled away. "Hey." His voice was gravelly, as if he'd just woken, but his eyes said he'd been up for a while.

"I received a letter from you about a month ago, saying that you would finally allow me to interview you. Can you tell me what spurred that change of mind?"

"I'm never going to see her again, so I guess I need to say my goodbye here. I told her not to come."

My poor, crazy son wanted to say goodbye to his mother, and he'd finally gotten his chance. I leaned forward in my seat, not wanting to miss a word. I'd never gotten a chance to say goodbye to my son. He hadn't let me say goodbye. At least I would finally hear him say it. My heart thudded in anticipation, my hands sweaty in my lap.

Sven asked, "Who's that? Your mother?"

Dane laughed. "*That old cow*? Nah. I'm talking about my Melissa."

I paused the video, not believing what I had just heard. I snapped my head around to Sven and snapped, "What is this? What did you make him say?"

"I didn't make him say anything. There's no coercion in his video. Everything Dane says is of his own accord. Let it play. You should hear what he has to say."

My eyes remained on Sven, trying more to see into him, to see the lies I knew he spoke. When I couldn't discern his motive, I turned back to the video and reluctantly started it again.

Sven's voice said, "And who's Melissa?" He sounded confused. I seconded that emotion.

"She's my *bitch*." At first, I hoped Dane meant "bitch" literally, as in a female dog, but in my gut, I knew differently. It wasn't the first time I'd heard my son cuss. He did plenty of that kind of thing just before he moved out of our house. Yet, I'd only heard him say such things in anger. The way he said that word in the video was flippant, as if it didn't matter that God was watching him.

Sven asked, "Care to elaborate on Melissa some more, Dane?"

"She's finer than fine. That girl is pretty, I tell you. I met her about the time I started hanging around Doc Morrow. She saw him, too, on occasion. I met her in Doc's lobby. That's before I killed all those people. I'm not a talking type, but the words just fell outta me. She was there to quit smoking. I was there because I wanted to hurt people. Guess Doc Morrow ain't very good, is he?" Dane erupted in guffaws. Tears twinkled in his eyes when he was done, the kind you get from laughing, not the sort brought on by sadness.

Under his breath, but loud enough for the high-tech microphone to catch, Video Sven said, "I guess not."

"Doc Morrow was nice, though. He did a lot for me, even though he didn't manage to calm my urges none. He made me realize that you don't hurt the ones you love. And 'cause of that, I found out my daddy never loved me." Dane's face went rigid, as if he smelled something resembling a sewer. "So that means Momma never loved me, neither. How could she've? She let Daddy hurt me. She let Daddy take my teeth."

I was full on bawling after that comment. I didn't give two shakes that Sven was present. I couldn't believe my baby boy had left the world thinking I didn't love him. Why would I have shown up for every trial if I didn't? I was there for him. I had to catch myself because I was fit to yell that thought directly at the TV, but with a few dirty words thrown in for good measure.

My heart skipped a beat, then sped up into my throat like a shuttle launching from Cape Canaveral. I recalled the words Dane had said while standing beside the sink: "Doc Morrow says the teeth might lead me home."

I'd had no idea who Doc Morrow was, and Dane had never mentioned him to me. I stared at Dane on the TV, professing his love for this Melissa woman, but I was out of the moment. If I didn't know about his shrink, then there was no way that the visions I'd been having of Dane were simple memories. Oh God, I'd been so wrong. Dane wasn't a memory. Dane meant to haunt me.

My son appeared beside the TV, his hands shaped like pistols. He fired both at me and winked as if to say, "She's finally got it." Then he disappeared.

I came up out of my chair. "Get out of my house!"

Sven, looking suddenly scared and very nervous, put his cup on my coffee table. "But you haven't seen—"

"Leave the gosh-darned thing. Get out!"

"Fine. Calm down. I'll leave."

"Get!"

"But he gave me this. Dane, that is." Sven approached me timidly, like a child coming to a whipping. He dug into his pants pocket and pulled out a folded piece of college-ruled notebook paper. He held it out like a peace offering. "He wanted this video to go to Melissa. His reasoning is on the tape. But, I-I thought you'd want to talk to her."

I snatched the paper from Sven's hand, crumpled it up, and threw it into the seat of Phil's recliner. Something hot was pressing against the inside of my right thigh. For a moment, I thought I might've peed myself again. I looked down and saw a large brown stain on the lower section of my pink sundress. I couldn't figure it out until I noticed the discarded mug on the carpet. I'd spilled hot coffee on myself and hadn't even noticed.

When I looked back up, Sven was no longer in sight. I heard the front door shut, marking his departure.

I turned back to the TV. "Oh, Dane…"

Dane was still talking, describing his Melissa to an unseen Sven Gödel. Not one mention of his tormented mother. Not a single word about me other than that bovine reference.

I reached down and picked up my coffee cup. I threw it at Phil's prized television, and the device wailed in protest—a shriek befitting a banshee of lore. The spider-webbed crack the cup had left in the screen stared back at me. Then, I realized the caterwauling hadn't come from the TV.

I was a mother, so I instinctually grabbed the phone off its base before running out onto the porch. Frank and Stanley were coming around the side of the house. Frank helped the wounded man along with an arm around Stanley's back.

I went to meet them. "What happened?"

"Big dumb"—and a few extra choice words I didn't care to focus on—"stuck himself with a screwdriver tryin' to open a can of paint," Frank blurted in one big breath.

Stanley held out his arm, and I gasped. The tool had gone in directly behind his thumb on his left hand. The screwdriver was buried to the hilt, lengthwise, and I could see the raised flesh that covered the shaft like a pink cloth draped over a pencil.

I chewed back some sick and said, "My Lord! Do you want me to call an ambulance?" I held up the phone, as if to prove I could perform the action I promised.

"Best, I think," Frank said.

Stanley sobbed. "You just don't want me bleeding in your truck."

"Screw you, man." Frank looked at me, as if he needed my approval over Stanley's. "I ain't that coldhearted."

I dialed 9-1-1 and pressed the phone to my ear.

Frank said, "How'd you manage to do it, is what I'm wanting to know."

"I knelt over, trying to get that lid pried off, when I felt someone watching me…"

"Well Being 9-1-1, how may I direct your call?" the dispatch person asked into my ear, but she sounded far away. I was paying more attention to Stanley's next words.

"… and when I looked up, there was this guy staring at me, cracking his knuckles. He…"

The dispatcher said, "Hello? Hello? Is anyone there?"

"… he was wearing an orange jumpsuit."

I dropped the phone and started backing away. I found myself looking in all directions, snapping my head left and right, trying to make sense of something that had no plausible explanation. The third painter stood at the corner of the house, wiping his face with a white handkerchief. He had a cigarette in one hand, and when he was done mopping his brow, he took a puff. He saw me looking at him. Pointing in Stanley and Frank's direction, he began shaking his head, as if to say, "Crazy so and so."

Frank hollered, "Hey, lady! What's wrong with you? Why'd you drop the phone? Hello? Stan, I think this woman went crazy on us."

Stanley said, "Sight of blood does that to some people. Grab the damn phone. This hurts like hell."

My head began to throb. The pain started in my temples and made its way up and around to the back of my head. *Thud, thud, thud.* A bass drum in my skull. Squinting my eyes against the pain, I still managed to see Frank scoop my phone out of the grass to finish talking to the dispatcher. I turned and headed for the house, intent on finding something to ease the pounding in my head.

I stopped in the middle of the yard, fear washing over me, as I looked at the front of my home.

Dane stood in my open front door, smiling. His hands played over each other. I could hear those knuckles popping in their sockets from a good fifty feet away.

TEN

DANE WAS SEVENTEEN WHEN HE left me alone with Phil. He'd finished his homeschooling with honors. I was a proud mother. I still worked for Rose Medical at that time and had just received my first raise in five years, and a substantial one at that. I came home that night, intent on bragging about how much money I'd be making and how we'd finally be able to pay off the credit cards.

Phil sat in his recliner, watching me pace across the living room while I spread my good news. Dane listened from the couch.

Dane had already grown into the behemoth of a man who would be executed thirteen years later. His thick, solid upper body was slumped forward, his elbows on his knees. He kept cracking his knuckles. He wasn't looking at me, though. He was staring at Phil, who was staring at me. Dane must've seen what was coming because I sure didn't.

Phil got up while I was in mid-sentence. I'd just reached the part about exactly how much my raise was. Phil stalked off into the kitchen, seemingly ignoring me.

"What's wrong with him?" I asked Dane.

Dane shrugged and slumped back into the sofa. Part of me thought all of Phil's anger and violence stemmed from our monetary situation. Our family had been in the red since the day we closed on our home. I always made sure Dane had brilliant birthdays and Christmases, but that took maxing out plastic to make it happen. Phil never complained about the excessive credit card bills. I figured he'd channeled his anger onto Dane. I imagined it as a vicious cycle. I'd buy things for Dane, trying to make up for Phil's abuse, which in turn, upset Phil even more. Or so it seemed.

Then, something shattered in the kitchen. Dane was up like a flash, but I was closer and had already made it to the kitchen door. Another crash sounded as I pushed open the door.

Phil stood at the cabinets. He had the door that lent access to my best china pulled open. Across the room lay shards of broken plates, where they'd been flung against the far wall.

Phil grabbed another plate and growled, "Damn bitch thinks she's better than me."

Maybe louder than I should have, I yelled, "What are you doing?"

Phil's actions clicked, and I understood. Up until that day, Phil had made more money than I did. He'd been a yardman for the railroad going on twenty years by then, was five years away from a nice retirement, and there his wife was, a woman, making a better wage. I'd challenged his manhood.

Phil moved in jerky, awkward movements across the expanse of the kitchen. I saw his left arm go up over his right shoulder but didn't realize what it meant. He backhanded me. My head swung around so quick and hard, I thought he'd broken my neck. I collapsed in the doorway, holding my throbbing face in my hands.

The air above me shifted, and through my splayed fingers, I saw Dane sail into the kitchen. The way my boy moved, I knew he meant to hurt Phil.

I sat and watched. I might have even smiled.

Dane grabbed the front of Phil's shirt in both fists and spun his father around, slamming him into the fridge. A great big breath came out of Phil in a *whoosh*! Phil clawed long, white lines in Dane's forearms that filled with blood an instant later. Dane reared back and shoved Phil into the refrigerator again. My son rolled to the side, his father still in his grasp, and tossed Phil across the kitchen like a shot-put.

Phil flew in what seemed like slow motion. My husband was still vertical, but his arms were out in front of him like a stalking Frankenstein. His legs stuck out as if he'd taken a seat on the floor. He hit the sliding glass door, back first, and the glass exploded. He landed in a heap on the back porch.

From his place by the fridge, Dane roared, "You don't touch her! You don't touch my momma!"

Dane walked past me then stopped in the doorway and looked down at me. A single tear rolled down his cheek. He slashed at it with one quick hand. The anger on his face bled away, and I was left looking at a scared child. He might have been seven again, standing there, looking for me to act. I jerked my throbbing chin in the direction of the front door. Dane stalked away, seeming twice as big as he had just moments before finally striking back at his father. I heard the front door slam. I supposed he left me there with his battered father because he was afraid he'd killed the man. Maybe not. Perhaps he left because I'd motioned for him to go. It took everything I had not to go after him, but I figured, at the very least, I owed him an unchallenged escape.

I didn't talk to Dane again after that, didn't even know how to reach him. I saw him during the trials, but we never shared any words.

I helped Phil up out of the pile of glass and to a kitchen chair. He remained silent while I pulled shards from his skin and disinfected the wounds with peroxide. All the vehemence had left the man. I had once seen Phil as some invincible, hulking beast, something I didn't threaten for fear that he would end me. He looked like a sulking child after Dane got through with him, his hardened shell chiseled away. I didn't feel sorry for him. I felt sorry for myself. I'd been so terrified of Phil, and for what? All that remained inside me was the Christian I'd become. I'd do the right thing and mend my husband, whether I cared about him or not.

When I finished tending to him, Phil gently took my wrist and petted my hand. "I'm sorry. You think he'll be back?"

"For your sake," I told him, "I hope not."

ELEVEN

FRANK AND THE UNNAMED PAINTER finished my wall after the paramedics left with Stanley.

I stood in my living room after the painters left, staring at the cracked frontage of Phil's television. I had another TV on the dresser in my room, but I didn't know if I wanted to see the rest of Dane's message. I wondered how my son had gone from being so protective of me to damning the air I breathed. Something had changed inside him at one point or another, but I was blind as to when that switch had occurred. I fancied a thought that maybe that Melissa woman had turned my son against me. But what reasoning could she have had? I'd never so much as heard her name before Sven Gödel brought me that video.

Confused and seeking answers, I disconnected the DVD player from Phil's set and walked with it, cables and all, into my bedroom. I plugged everything in before going back to the living room for the remote.

When I returned, I lay on my belly on the bed, my head at the end, pillows stuffed under my chest. I turned on the TV and the player with their respective remotes, then started the video.

I had no need to hear that cow reference again, so I fast-forwarded to Dane's description of Melissa. He went into glorious detail about his love, a woman I'd never known even existed.

On the screen, Dane cracked his knuckles. "You're going to take this tape to my Melissa, right?"

Off-camera, Sven responded, "I can, yes."

"That's real good. Not that I could do anything about it if you didn't, but she's probably a might worried about my mood in here. I'm going to talk to her now, if you don't mind." Dane's polite attitude was startling. I didn't feel as though I was hearing the words of a killer, but that of my wonderful baby boy.

Video Sven said, "Be my guest, Dane."

Dane looked deep into the camera and his rough countenance softened. "Hey, Mimi. I guess I'm okay. Been hearing some from Doc Morrow. Not the real guy, but the one that's in my head. You know what I'm talking about. He says you were good for me. He tells me that when I smell cinnamon, it's you thinking about me 'cause of the way you always smelled like the stuff. Bully—he's my cellie—says that cinnamon isn't really cinnamon, that it's this bark-like stuff. They don't sell real cinnamon cheap, so they use this other stuff, the bark stuff, to make it. It's called Kasha, or Kashi, or something like that. But I smell it when I think of you. Helps me relax a bit. Maybe you can put some cinnamon or Kasha-whatever on my grave after they kill me. That way I could always smell you."

Dane's eyes dripped tears. The sight destroyed me. My heart hurt. I rolled over onto my side and began rubbing my chest, right between my breasts.

"Well, Mimi, I think that's it. I told this reporter guy that he could ask me some questions as long as I got to talk to you. You take care of yourself." Dane sniffled. He rubbed snot from his nose with the back of one hand and wiped gunk onto the stomach of his orange jumpsuit. He looked off camera and said, "You got questions? Shoot."

"Only a few." I heard the rustling of paper in the camera's mic. "Can you tell me why you killed the people you did?"

"My daddy knocked me around when I was growing up is what you're wanting to hear, right? That I had a horrible childhood that got so bad it broke something in my mind that controls my actions, right? But that's not all true. I get these urges. I go to this place where people don't look right. They're all smiley, and their teeth are so gosh-darn big and ugly I just gotta take 'em. So I did."

"Why men *and* women?"

"Because they're what I could find. I knew what I was doing, Mister. Make no bones about that. Like I told the investigators what interviewed me, I waited 'til those rest stops were empty. Sometimes, they'd be empty when I got there, and other times, they'd be full. If I didn't get a chance 'cause there were too many people around, I just moved along to my next spot. I had a job to do. East-Western needed their products moved, so I had to make good. I got my work ethic from my bitch of a mother. She always did love work more than she loved me."

Dane had been looking away, I assumed at Sven, to answer the questions. He suddenly focused directly on the camera and said, "You don't let my momma nowhere near you, Mimi. She's not good news."

I paused the DVD. I'd never get used to hearing my son call me such things. I got up and grabbed the

Kleenex from the bathroom. I was starting to soak my pillow. I felt as if a rodent had scurried into my brain pan. I could sense that rat rummaging around in there, messing with my lucid thoughts, jumbling them all up. I could make no sense of Dane's hatred for me, but I ruled out Melissa as a suspect. If he was trying to tell her not to come near me, then it was unlikely she was the person who turned Dane against me. I was back at square one.

The unknown-to-me Doc Morrow flitted into my mind, and that scavenging rodent ate him alive. No psychiatrist would ever implant bad thoughts into a patient's head. The thought seemed abhorrent, so I dismissed it. There was nothing to gain from turning a patient against his mother. Of that, I was certain. I steeled myself and pressed Play.

Video Sven asked, "So you took people's teeth because they looked *different* to you?"

"That about sums it up." Dane chuckled and cracked his knuckles. "People don't always look bad, though. My spells only come about a couple times a year. Mostly when I've been on the road too long and I haven't seen my Melissa."

"Did Melissa know the entire time?"

"Know what?" Dane seemed genuinely confused.

"That you killed people."

"Oh, that!" Dane waved Sven off with a loose flop of his wrist. The nonchalant response made my stomach churn. "Not until I was caught. She'd seen me acting different at times and always asked what was wrong. I just told her my brain wasn't working right. That I had too much up here." He tapped his temple.

I knew exactly how he felt.

Video Sven asked, "Did Melissa ever look odd to you? Did you ever want to take her teeth, Dane?"

"Gosh, no. My Melissa's different. That's how come I love her so much. When I'm with her, man, I don't see nothin' wrong with the world. She's like this veil, right? Like I can't see the bad stuff when she's around. We'll screw around, and the world will come to a standstill, you know? She calls it making love, but I'm not as digitized as her."

"Do you mean 'dignified,' Dane?"

"Yeah, that word. I swear, my Melissa is God's way of telling me that there's right in the world. I'd never have hurt her because there's not a bad bone in her whole body. Not to sound sappy, man, but she's everything a guy like me looks for in a woman. Completely different from my mother. I don't know what my daddy ever saw in that bitch."

That nasty word coming from my only child's mouth, especially in reference to me, stopped my breathing. For the second time, I wondered what I had done to deserve his apparent hatred.

On the screen, Dane continued talking, spilling out more disgusting names for me. Every time he mentioned me, he looked as though he had something awful stuck in his mouth, as if he were chewing excrement and couldn't get the junk to go down.

I imagined I could taste the same mess on my own tongue. I pulled my ashtray and cigarettes off the nightstand, lit a Virginia Slim, and went back to watching my son cuss me.

Thankfully, Sven changed the subject. "Do you regret killing any of those people, Dane?"

"I don't feel bad about a single one of 'em. I liked it. Every time I got home to my Melissa afterwards, she'd always ask me what had got me so dag-blasted happy all of a sudden. We had this thing where I'd kiss her on the forehead and she'd kiss my chest. It's how we came together after a haul. We'd stay like that forever, with God in his heaven and my angel in my arms. I never had no thought of marryin' her, though. Didn't want to end up like my folks, you know? She never made no inklin' that I should ask, so I never did. We didn't need no piece of paper to tell us we shared something beautiful. The proof was in the happenin', right? Or puddin'. Or however that saying goes. All I know is, we was something special." Dane looked into the camera. "I miss you, Mimi."

"Dane, I can't help but notice sometimes you call her 'your Melissa,' and other times you call her 'Mimi.' Why is that?"

"Because you gotta understand when I'm talkin' to you that she's mine. When I'm talkin' to her, she already knows she belongs to me, so I can call her what I like."

"So Melissa was your property?"

"And I was hers."

"Do you think Melissa would like knowing you consider her an item to be owned, Dane?"

"What the hell you trying to get at, man?"

"Nothing, nothing. I just want to make sure that you don't upset Melissa when I show her this tape."

Dane's eyes, stricken with anger, honed in on Sven off camera. I thought I could see that killer then, the one who resided in my child, always hidden away until Dane needed him. I took a puff off my Slim and leaned in closer to the TV.

Dane growled, "I don't like your tone, man."

"I didn't mean anything by it, Dane. I think we can stop here. Is that all right?"

Dane stood and leaned across the table, but his shackles saved Sven from Dane getting too close. "You're not going to turn me in the eyes of my Melissa, shit for brains. She's all the good I got left. You make me look bad, man, and I'll find you, somehow, and rip those teeth straight from your smirking head!"

I flicked my ash into the tray. When I looked back at the screen, Dane was staring directly into the camera. His face was as still as water in a bathtub.

From the television, Dane said, "You really do need to quit smoking, Momma."

I couldn't grab the remote fast enough. I jammed my thumb onto the power button, and the screen went black. My heart felt fit to explode. I put out my cigarette, set the ashtray on the floor, and rolled over onto my back to alleviate the pressure from my chest.

Seven-year-old Dane spider-crawled across the ceiling, making circles around my spinning fan blades. He grinned at me, his mouth a black void. Teeth fell out of that vacant hole and rained down over my body. Torrents of canines and molars, bicuspids and wisdom teeth tried to bury me alive.

I screamed. Fistfuls of teeth landed in my mouth. Spitting and gagging, I rolled off the bed. I landed on my hands and knees. Scurrying away from the amassing pile of teeth, I could hear Dane giggling above me.

I hit the hallway and pulled myself to my feet against one wall. Stupid me looked back and found Dane laughing in the door to my bedroom. He'd grown into an adult again. His orange jumper glowed in the light radiating from my room.

"The teeth'll lead me home, Momma. And when I'm done, won't be no running left to do."

I pried my eyes off Dane with effort and ran. I ended up spilling over Phil's recliner, upending the thing and myself along with it. I crashed down into the middle of the living room and slid face-first in the carpet, burning my cheek on the piling. I yelped. The entire right side of my face felt as though it was on fire. Rolling over, I kicked the overturned chair out of my way so I could look down the hall.

He was gone. Thank God in heaven, Dane was gone.

A small white spot nearby caught my eye. It sat lonely like a pale island in a sea of brown rug. I reached for it, picked it up, and pulled apart the crumpled, college-ruled paper.

Melissa Dugan
117 East Ninth Street
Apartment 10
Roanoke, Virginia 24013

A phone number was scrawled beneath the address. Somehow, those words and numbers calmed me. It was something to focus my attention on. Even without proof to back up my theory, I hoped that maybe if I didn't think about Dane, he'd just leave me alone. I prayed he was gone for the evening. He'd had his fun, or whatever it was he thought he was doing to me. I got to my feet and walked into the kitchen. I meant to dial Melissa's phone number right then and there, but as I reached for the phone, I noticed the blinking message light. When Sven had called the day before to set up our meeting, there'd been four messages. I still hadn't listened to them, but the display showed five.

Still out of breath from my scare and tumble, I willed my breathing back to normal. Everything was coming to light, but I suddenly wished I was back in the dark. Not knowing, not understanding, and thinking that Dane was a simple hallucination had been so reassuring. I didn't have a clue what I was up against, only that I was up against *something*, and that knowledge scared me stupid.

I put the notebook page under a magnet on the fridge door before pressing Play on the answering machine.

The first four messages were Sven telling me to call him back, that he needed to meet with me, so I deleted each one until I made it to the fifth.

The voice sounded garbled, as if the person were under water or using some kind of electronic voice filter. "We're watching you, Ella May Peters. They should kill—"

I pressed Delete so hard I bent the nail on my index finger back to the quick. I didn't have to hear the rest of the message. I'd read it full and well when they'd painted it on the side of my house. My heart raced. I prayed. Oh, how I prayed. God would see that I made it out of my current situation. He'd seen me through many hard times. I only needed to rely on Him.

I found Officer Sherwood's card on the dining table where I'd left it. I got my pulse under control then dialed his number with a trembling finger. While phone rang in my ear, I wondered why I hadn't heard my own phone ringing over the past few days. I checked the ringer, but it was at full volume.

I felt my headache returning. I pulled down my Tylenol and took three of the white and red gel caps with a glass of water. Sherwood's voicemail answered. I left a message for him to contact me as soon as possible. I could've very well called 9-1-1 again but decided against it. Sherwood was already on the case, and I didn't want to have to explain everything to someone new. Besides, if someone meant me harm, I assumed he would have acted already. I figured the person was only trying to scare me.

I dumped the remainder of my water into the sink and set the glass in the dish rack. When I turned back to the sink, I shrieked.

A pile of teeth clogged the drain. All around me, I heard Dane laughing.

Bracing myself on the lip of the sink, I closed my eyes and prayed.

TWELVE

DANE DIDN'T COME OUT OF diapers until he was four and a half years old. Even then, he had frequent accidents well past the age of five. His pediatrician—we had one before Phil saw fit to keep Dane bruised up on a constant basis—thought Dane suffered from night terrors. But I attributed it to daytime horrors.

One weekend afternoon in particular, Phil and I were watching a special on anemia. Though I couldn't remember how we landed on such a program, the show seemed to interest Phil to no end. I never had much control over the remote, so on that channel we stayed. Five-year-old Dane had been playing on the back porch with his Lego set. During a commercial, Dane came running inside. Phil was a staunch supporter of no running in the house, so before Dane could get to the hallway, Phil yelled and stopped the boy in his tracks.

"What the hell are you doing? What did I say about running in the house?"

"I gotta go potty."

I believe the smell hit Phil and me about the same time. My nose curled up until I squinted, and Phil's face twitched spastically as if he were going through a seizure.

Phil asked, "You crap yourself?"

"Nuh-nuh-no, sir." Dane looked meek, tiny.

"Don't lie to me. You did, didn't you? I can smell you, Dane!" Phil roared his final words as he rose from his recliner.

On instinct, I came out of the loveseat and moved to protect Dane.

Phil turned, laid his hand between my breasts, and shoved me back down onto the couch. "I got this, Ella."

Phil backed Dane into the corner of the living room, just beside the entrance to the hallway. Dane cowered before his hulking father, already crying and begging Phil not to hurt him. Phil grabbed Dane's left ear and twisted until the boy dropped to his knees. Phil pulled Dane back up and led him through the kitchen to the sliding glass door.

I managed to build up enough courage to follow about thirty seconds later. When I stepped out onto the back porch, Dane was sitting on one of the bench seats attached to the picnic table in the backyard. Phil stood over him, one hand on Dane's shoulder, pushing the child down into the wood of the bench.

Phil growled, "You sit in your filth, little boy, and you think about what you done. Them darn blocks, them *LEGOs*, ain't that important. You gotta crap, you stop what you're doing, and you crap. You understand me?" Only, of course, Phil used much more colorful language.

Dane nodded with fervor, his chest hitching with sobs and labored breaths.

"Now, you're gonna sit there, in your nasty, and think about what you done. I'll come get you when you can get up." Phil left Dane on the bench and walked across the yard toward me. "That'll teach him," Phil said as he passed me.

I said, "Don't you think we should clean him—"

My head jerked back, and my scalp lit on fire. Phil wrenched my hair until I was looking up at him, my neck fit to snap.

Phil hissed like a snake. "You handle the comfort, Ella. I'll handle the *goddamned* discipline." Phil had a way of blaspheming that would make God himself want to crawl inside a hole to get away.

Phil let me go and stormed back into the house. He left the sliding glass door open so he could holler back at me, "I mean for you to come back and watch the rest of this show with me, Ella!"

I stared at Dane, lost in his eyes. My son's face was soaked with tears. He just kept shaking his head, knowing it wouldn't be good for him if he spoke but willing me with his eyes to do something. I did something, all right. I left him on that bench and went back to the tragedy of anemia.

The blood disorder program went off, and Phil changed the station to one of the paid movie channels. I could remember explosions and loads of action, Phil hooting and hollering about how fantastic the special effects were, but I couldn't recall the name of the film or anyone who starred in it. I sat next to my husband, the TV blaring, and thought about Dane sitting out there, marinating in the foulness contained in his pants. I wanted to say something to Phil so badly that my entire body felt heavy from the weight of the unsaid words. But I remained as quiet as a mouse.

A cool breeze came in through the kitchen. I'd left the door open so I could hear Dane, should he call for me. What I did hear was sniffling, even over the roar of the action movie. I couldn't see my son, and that hurt just as bad as my inactivity.

The flick rolled credits, and Phil got up. My heart leapt. Finally, he was going to let Dane come in and get clean. Only Phil didn't head in the direction of the back door. Instead, he went to the bathroom, where I heard him urinate forcefully into the bowl. He'd left the door open, more than likely because he wanted to make sure I didn't go check on Dane or offer any comfort.

When Phil returned, he changed the channel to the afternoon news. He cussed a talking-head who reported on the president's plans to raise taxes.

The sun went down. Phil had me cook fried chicken with baked potatoes. I sat at the kitchen table while I did so and husked corn like an automaton. Thoughts of leaving Phil and taking Dane with me crossed my mind, but I'd just started working for Rose Medical, and my tenure was still three years in the future. Dane and I couldn't survive on our own, I thought, along with several other stupid excuses. So I prepared our meal in silence.

When it was ready to serve, Phil came into the kitchen with a bath towel draped over his arm. He set the stove to two hundred degrees and told me to put the food inside to keep it warm.

"Let's go," he said, handing me the towel.

I followed him out and stood on the porch while Phil stripped Dane naked in the middle of the backyard. We didn't have a privacy fence, or a fence of any nature, so I was surprised our neighbors didn't say something to me later. Perhaps they never saw the spectacle. Phil took Dane's clothing, holding them out in front of him and pinching his nose with his free hand, around the side of the house. I heard the trash bin's lid rise and fall with a creak and thump. Phil came back and went straight for the garden hose. I reached for Phil, trying to will him not to do what I knew was coming, but was unable to speak.

Phil turned the spigot on full blast. He approached Dane, who was hugging himself, and let the sprayer on the end of the hose go full-rip. The force of the stream put divots in Dane's flesh. My son cried out in shock and began shivering. Even at five years old, he took his punishment and didn't run. He knew from experience that things would get much worse if he tried anything.

Phil shouted, "Turn around!"

Dane did as he was told, moving in a tight circle, his feet doing all the work. Phil washed the caked feces from Dane's backside. Then, Phil bent, placed his hand on Dane's butt cheeks, and splayed them apart so he could force the jet of water inside.

That was too much for my son. He squealed and shrieked, pedaling away from his father. Phil snatched him by the shoulder and pulled him back.

When the cleaning was done, Phil rolled up the hose. He called to me, "Your turn!"

I raced across the yard like a marathon runner who had heard a starter gun. I wrapped Dane's shivering form in the towel and began to gently massage him dry. Picking him up, I carried my sobbing child into the bathroom. After checking the spreading redness on his rear end, I applied some diaper rash ointment to the area. I'd seen plenty of neglected nursing home patients come to the hospital with bedsores. I couldn't let that happen to Dane. I'd already let too much go on that day.

Dane and I kneeled beside his bed and said the Lord's Prayer. Dane's voice was meek, barely audible even when I lowered my own voice to listen to make sure he was still reciting the words.

I tacked on an extra bit before saying amen: "Please forgive Dane's father, Lord, for he knows not Your spirit."

When I opened my eyes, Dane was staring up at me and shaking his head. I tried to tell myself that Dane was too young to realize what a failure I'd been to him, but I could see the understanding already present in his dull eyes. A light had died in there. He no longer looked at me like a mother, but as a prisoner of war would look at a doctor who meant to keep him alive between torture sessions.

THIRTEEN

THE DAY OF TALIA STEMSFORD'S fundraiser, I drove into town extra carefully. I hadn't seen Dane in two weeks, but the last thing I needed was him popping up while I was behind the wheel. If my dead son appeared in the passenger seat, I would probably drive into a gas station pump to meet a fiery end or run my car through the guardrail on Watercourse Crossway to plummet into the depths of Lake Rosenthal.

I pulled into the parking lot of Well Being Public Library around nine o'clock that morning. Talia's red minivan was the only other car in the area. She had already set up two ten-foot folding tables on the sidewalk by the road. Behind the makeshift seller's booth was the library, a two-story brick cube that had been around since the early 1920s.

I got out of the car, locking the door behind me, and took the wraparound walkway up to the glass frontage of the building. Talia was coming out of the double doors she'd propped open, a tall stack of books nestled in her arms.

"Hey, there!" she squealed. "I'm so glad you made it."

"The note you left on the calendar said nine. Did you need me earlier?"

"Really? I thought I wrote seven. My penmanship isn't always so good. Oh well. Better late than never, eh?"

I smiled. "I suppose. Here, let me have those."

I took the fifteen-odd books from her, and she adjusted her pink silk blouse. Dust from the old books had left gray lines in horizontal patterns across her chest and stomach. I kept the books away from my own shirt.

"How old are these things?" I asked.

"Not really all that much. They've just been in storage. What with Julia and Kimberly being out because of the new baby, I haven't had much time to dust that back room."

Julia Oldman was Kimberly's mother. The pair worked the library on Talia's off days. I had met both women on many occasions, but the last time I had seen them was before Dane's death. I hadn't even known Kimberly was pregnant.

"The father's not involved with the child," Talia said as she led me to the tables. "Sperm donor, you know."

My cheeks grew hot, and I felt foolish for it. I was a Christian woman, not a prude, but Talia's name for the father caused me to imagine a man between a woman's legs with a turkey-baster.

Talia continued while she helped me sort the books into three piles. "Julia went to part time and only works four hours on Wednesdays and the five hours we're open on Saturday. Other than that, it's just little ol' me."

"I wish I could help more, but—"

"Oh, deary, no. I'm not trying to guilt trip you. I'm just bringing you up to speed. Gotta gossip, right? You know how us girls do." She laid a hand on my shoulder and smiled.

Talia and I went back up the walkway and into the library. The smell of aged paper—that vanilla scent I'd come to cherish over five and a half decades of escaping into literature—soothed me. I wished I had time to read more, but with Dane's uncanny appearances and all the craziness with those people harassing me, I just couldn't focus long enough to become immersed in a story.

As if reading my mind, Talia said, "I heard about the graffiti. Awful mess, dear."

We turned right into the foyer and passed a bulletin board laden with activities. A notice told that Friday Night Story Time would be cancelled until the library was better staffed. Kimberly used to handle that assignment. Sometimes, after Phil died, I would come and join the party just to get out of the empty house.

We stepped into the main area of the library. The checkout desk sat on the left, and bookshelves ran away in long strides all the way to the back of the building. Pole lights hung from the ceiling, steel cones casting rays of golden light over the room. I'd always considered libraries magical places. Walking inside one was like going to a train station, and I likened picking out a book to jumping onto a passenger car without bothering to check the destination.

Continuing our conversation, I told Talia, "The vandals called me two weeks ago. Left me a rather creepy message about how they were watching me."

Talia accentuated her shock with a palm over her heart. "No! They didn't!"

"Yes, they most certainly did. I called the officer in charge of the investigation and left him a message."

Talia took me to a book cart that must have had a hundred volumes stacked on it. "It won't roll over the kick plate inside the foyer, so I left it here. With your help, I think we might could lift it. So did the policeman call you back?"

"Yeah. The next day. He said there wasn't much he could do."

"And why not?" Talia sounded so comically upset that I almost laughed at her.

"I deleted the message. Not a whole lot they could do with no proof. He said he would check with the phone company, but he still hasn't gotten back to me. Either way, I destroyed the evidence, so all he'll have is a possible phone number."

"That's atrocious! Surely there's *something* they can do."

"I don't think these people—whoever they are— mean me any harm. They're just upset over Dane. Or maybe Officer Sherwood is right. Maybe it's just kids goofing off."

Talia began pushing the cart toward the hallway of the foyer. I helped on my corner. Together, we lifted it over the kickplate.

She said, "Officer Sherwood, huh?"

"That's the one."

"He had a crush on me, once upon a time. I think he'd handcuff me if I gave him half a chance." She winked at me.

"Talia Stemsford, you minx." I laughed. It felt good.

"How long's it been, Ella? Since, you know…" She nudged my elbow with her own.

"I'm sure I wouldn't tell you even if I remembered."

"That long? Deary, you need to get laid. And soon!"

We both settled into a fit of laughter. I stopped pushing the cart to catch my breath.

In between giggles, I said, "And you call yourself… a religious woman?"

"We all find joy in the touch of a man." Talia wiped tears from the corners of her eyes, being mindful of her eyeliner while she did. "The Lord made the act pleasurable so we'd be fruitful and multiply."

"I guess so."

The last time Phil had taken me to bed was before he'd gotten sick. That was over ten years in the past, and our coitus had been brief and unsatisfying. I couldn't recall if Phil had even orgasmed. Before Dane, making love to Phil had been a pleasurable experience. For all his faults, Phil knew how to please a woman. After Dane was born, our sex life dwindled down to a once a month thing, something done out of necessity on Phil's part and respect on mine. He was my husband, and he should not want. When Dane got older and the beatings began, Phil hadn't exactly forced himself on me, but he didn't seem to care whether or not I enjoyed our coupling, either. I'd become nothing more than a hole to be filled.

My thoughts killed my laughter, so I placed my hands back on the cart and began to push again. Only it didn't budge.

"Let me help." Talia pushed her side, and together, we failed miserably. "What in the world?"

I shrugged. "Maybe the carpet's caught the wheels."

"I'll see." She pulled up her jean skirt a little and knelt down in front of the cart.

I watched over her shoulder. She splayed her hand over the carpet by the wheels then tugged at something wedged between the carpet fibers and the caster. She brought it up to the light and shrieked.

The tiny brown speck bounced around on the threadbare carpet like a bean on a trampoline until it came to rest beside the open double doors.

Shock and confusion anchored me to the floor. Sitting in the daylight coming through the library's doors was a molar caked in dried, rust-colored blood.

Talia offered her explanations, and I listened, feeling numb. She surmised that someone had kept the tooth in his pocket and, while rummaging for keys or something, had inadvertently dropped the tooth into the carpet, where it had stayed until we'd found it. I didn't ask her why someone would be walking around with a molar in his pants, but she filled me in on her guess, anyway.

"Maybe a kid lost it the night before, and when the mom pulled it out from under the kid's pillow, she just stuffed it in her jeans. You know, playing tooth fairy."

I made no attempt to explain that the tooth was definitely from an adult. I'd had my wisdom teeth removed when I was nineteen, and the tooth Talia had found looked exactly like one of those.

"Think I should call the cops?" she asked.

"What? Why?" I didn't tell her that I was sure the tooth would disappear before the authorities arrived. "I thought you said you were sure it came from some parent."

"I'm not *sure* of anything. But maybe we should."

"There's no crime scene. It's just a tooth. We'd be embarrassed as all get-out if you were right with your first guess."

"Well, there's…" She trailed off, looking me up and down.

I could see the accusation in her eyes, the cold judgment, and I almost wanted to slap her. "What? Some connection with *Dane*? Don't start that with me, Talia. I've got enough on my plate."

"Right, right. Oh, dear. What was I thinking? I'm so sorry. I'm being foolish, aren't I? Here, let me get rid of it." She jogged back into the main room of the library and returned a moment later with a box of generic-brand tissues. She pulled one out and picked up the tooth with it, then she threw the crumpled tissue with the molar inside into the trash receptacle by the front door.

She dusted her hands together. "That's that, then. Out of sight, out of mind."

I couldn't have agreed with her more. Even though I couldn't see the molar any longer, I still felt out of my mind.

Well Being had a population of ten thousand and some change. Either Talia hadn't promoted the fundraiser well enough or people just didn't care because only twenty-some-odd folks showed up for the event. Plus, it was Sunday, and the library should've been closed, so I assumed most people were in church or simply enjoying the last day of the weekend.

Talia met each would-be customer with a smile and a handshake, or a hug for the ones she knew well enough. I sat behind the tables with a money box in my lap, collecting cash from those who saw fit to buy some of the library's oldest books.

A young blond woman dressed in jeans and a Ravens jersey approached Talia just after three o'clock and asked to use the restroom. In that section of town, there was only the Baptist church across the street and the city hall next door — both of which were closed — so the library had the only available restroom within walking distance. Talia took the woman into the building.

Talia came back a minute later and sat back down next to me. "How much have we made?"

"Around forty bucks, but most of that was off those kids whose mother looked `bout ready to explode from hyperactive overload."

"Yes, I remember the dear. Her name's Porter."

I laughed. "Is that her first name?"

Talia nodded. "Don't ask. Her father owns the Den, and her husband is the bartender."

"Gotcha."

"Are you a drinking woman, Ella?"

The question caught me off guard. "Why?"

"Because I've been wondering if a few nips before bed will help me sleep better. I keep having these nightmares about bats. Nasty things. Never have liked them."

"Something bringing this on? I mean, anything wrong?"

"I stopped going door-to-door for the church, you know."

"No, I didn't know."

"Well, I did. And, deary, let me tell you, they were none too pleased with me. So I stopped going to church on Saturdays."

I had to remind myself that Jehovah's Witnesses considered Sundays the Sabbath, much like Christians, but JWs were much more strict. A believer shouldn't plan anything for Sunday, not even church, so they attended services on Saturdays instead.

"Ever since I stopped, the bad dreams have come back."

"*You're* not going to church?"

"Being that you're here today, Ella, I see *you're* not, either."

I didn't feel the need to rehash my encounter with Meredith Pearce at Well Being First Baptist, so I said, "I'll give you that. But I had to help out a friend who didn't ignore me when she found out my son was a murderer."

"Thank you. I do appreciate it more than you'll ever know." She leaned toward me and wrapped her arms around my shoulders.

Without planning on it, I hugged her back. Whether or not she was another woman happened to be a moot point. I enjoyed the feel of her warmth. I hadn't realized until then how much I missed human contact.

I found myself looking over Talia's shoulder while we embraced, scanning the area for Dane. I didn't know what rules applied to my apparition of a son. Whether or not he would pop up in public was something that kept me concerned.

We packed everything away just after five p.m. I helped Talia load the book cart again. On our way in, I felt nature's call. "I'm gonna run to the little girl's room."

She didn't really need my help pushing the cart. A couple who said they collected old novels had arrived around a quarter past four and lightened the load by more than thirty books. I put their hundred dollar bill in the money box, but when I tried to give them their thirty bucks in change, they told me to keep it.

Talia nodded. "Sure thing. I'll just put these back in storage. I'll wait for you at the doors."

I half-walked, half-ran around the circulation desk in the middle of the great room. The restrooms were located in the very back of the building, between the Ki-Le and Le-Ma fiction stacks. I passed King and Koontz, along with Lehane and McDonald, on my way to empty my bladder.

As I pushed through the door, the smell slapped me in the face. I'd changed many bedpans and dirty diapers—for the elderly, the disabled, and my own child—so I was accustomed to the reek of bowel movement, no matter the subtle differences. But that smell of week-old refuse, with a pinch of over-ripe banana, caused me to gag.

The young woman in the Ravens jersey sat against the far wall, leaning against a closed stall door. She was naked from the waist down. Her jeans were in a muddy mess in one corner. Her legs spastically worked her feet through a puddle of excrement.

She looked up at me with tear-filled eyes. "I-I-I couldn't g-g-get the d-d-door open. The st-stalls wouldn't open. The sink won't work. I-I couldn't get out. I scr-screamed, b-b-but no one came. I cou-couldn't help it."

To the blond woman's right, a stall door creaked open. Dane sat on the commode, cracking his knuckles.

"Practice makes perfect, Momma. I'm getting stronger. Soon, the teeth'll lead me home."

The woman reached for me with brown hands. The world tilted. I braced myself inside the frame of the restroom's doorway. The sight of the woman and Dane's presence in the stall was all too much. I vomited all over myself.

FOURTEEN

IN THE CASE OF FREDERICKA Devereau, Dane's pro-bono attorney, Mr. Isley, let Dane take the stand. That was a mistake. At least *I* saw it that way. I couldn't help but think that if Dane hadn't recounted his actions the night of September 8, 2005, he might not have been put to death. Sure, he'd have remained in the custody of the state for the rest of his life, but he wouldn't have been dead.

Dane took the stand. He began cracking his knuckles. I sat two rows back on the left side, a good forty feet from my son, yet I could still hear the joints popping in his hands.

Mr. Isley, a gray-haired man with a potbelly and elf-like ears, started with, "Can you please tell us what happened the night of Fredericka Devereau's death, Dane?"

Dane cleared his throat. He grasped the wooden top of the stand in front of him and rolled his neck as if he were getting ready for strenuous activity. Then, he leaned back and said, "I waited in my truck for four hours before she come along. The rest area had cleared out about two in the morning, three hours after I'd pulled in. That girl" — Dane never called his victims by name, something I'd learned most serial killers didn't do because it would have made their victims people instead of bodies—"she come along in a white Oldsmobile older than I was. The backfire coming out of the muffler is what got my attention. I was reading the back of *A Christmas Carol*, that section what tells you about the story, the whole reason I bought that book in the first place, and *blewy*! come that tail pipe. I don't remember much about the girl—"

Isley cut in, "Fredericka Devereau?"

"Yeah, her. Don't even recall what she looks like. I seen her go into the little girls' room inside my backin'-up mirrors, you know, and I jumped down out of the cab to go wait on her. When she came out, I was waitin'. I snatched her up by the throat, and her eyes got all big. Don't remember what color her eyes were, though."

"That's all right, Dane. Please, tell us how she made you feel."

Dane grimaced. I thought I saw regret in his eyes, and I was sure that was why Isley put him on the stand in the first place, but then the compassion train went off the rails. Dane laughed. "I felt alive."

Isley's back was to me, but I saw his body go rigid. "That's not what you told me, Dane. Please, tell the court what you told me."

"I've been thinking about what I told you, Isley, and I don't think I was bein' honest with you. I thought I felt bad with her big ol' snow globes peering at me, but that weren't sadness I felt. Nope. That was anticipation."

"You told me looking at her made you sick, Dane."

I'd watched enough *Law & Order* in my day to expect that Prosecutor Parker should've jumped up and hollered something like, "Objection! Leading the witness, Your Honor," but he didn't. Dane was making

Parker's goal of a death sentence a possibility right before his eyes.

"You ever get excited 'til you puke, Isley? I know I do. That's why my stomach got to me. Felt bad? Pshah! It felt good. I drug her back to my truck and worked on her. That girl didn't scream. Not once. I think I crushed her voice box. Don't know, though. When I was done, I threw her up on the roof of the bathrooms, but I couldn't get her all the way up. I guess that's how they found her, her legs dangling over the edge like they were. Didn't need to leave anyone the trail that night, so I kept her teeth for my jar."

Isley's shoulders slumped. He turned to the judge. "That'll be all for my defendant, Your Honor."

When Isley turned around, he found my face in the crowd. He shook his head and shrugged, as if to say, "I did the best I could."

Prosecutor Parker took his turn. "Dane, can you tell us how exactly you were able to get a grown woman up onto an eight-foot-high building by yourself?"

"Oh, that were easy as pie."

Dane measured in at six-foot-three and weighed two-hundred-sixty pounds when he was caught. I knew how he'd gotten her up there, but I listened anyway.

"I grabbed her by the ankles, one in each hand, and twisted around as I come up." Dane stood. He walked around the side of the stand and stopped in the space between the attorney's tables and the judge's podium. Armed guards put their hands on their guns, left the far wall where they'd been standing, and began to approach Dane.

The judge waved a hand at them. "Allow him."

Dane bent over as if he were going to touch his toes, but grabbed two fistfuls of air instead. My mind filled in the blanks. I saw Fredericka's ankles clutched in Dane's bear-sized paws. Dane came up, twirling around as he did. Fredericka's air-body went with him, and she ended up upside down, her invisible stomach flush with Dane's rump as he held her imaginary legs over his head. Dane took two lunging steps forward, and swung away from himself, like a man breaking brick with a sledgehammer. Fredericka's air-body sailed through the courtroom and landed in a crumpled mess atop the judge's paperwork.

I shook my head to clear the image from my mind.

Dane said, "Took me only one time doing it. I got her up there, and there she stayed. Like I said, easy as pie."

Prosecutor Parker called up the image on the monitor of how Fredericka was found. Two legs dangled down over the top of the restroom's roof, directly in front of the hallway that lent access to the ladies' room. Fredericka had on pink sneakers and plaid Capri pants.

The picture reminded me of the Wicked Witch of the East, her ruby slippers and candy-striped stockings peeking out from under Dorothy's tornado-ravaged home.

FIFTEEN

WHEN I FOUND THE WOMAN in the Ravens jersey, I was surprised I didn't wet myself. I called for Talia, and she arrived to find me leaning against the sink and the woman in the Ravens jersey still wallowing in her own muck. Talia ran back to the checkout desk to grab the cordless phone, and when she returned, I went into the men's room to pee. Afterward, I tried my best to clean the front of my shirt off in the sink, but being that the facilities only had a hot air blower and no paper towels, my mess just became messier.

I went out and saw Talia standing in the doorway to the women's restroom. Peeking in, I noticed the woman had moved back to her place against the stalls. A thought occurred to me. Why hadn't she simply crawled under a stall to use a toilet? I'd never know, but I imagined I could guess why. Dane hadn't *allowed* her to. I could see, very clearly in my mind's eye, Dane grabbing the woman in the Ravens jersey by the ankles every time she tried to shimmy under a door. He would pull her back out. The process had repeated itself until the woman went mad and soiled the floor.

I stayed outside the restroom while Talia went to the front of the library to wait for the police and EMTs. I didn't own a watch, or cell phone, so time seemed to pass slowly. I kept the door closed but would peek in every few minutes to check on the woman. She continued to rock back and forth, crying.

Finally, Talia led a man and woman in light-blue paramedic garb into the back of the library. The female EMT was short, round, and heavy about the chest. She looked as if she could bench-press a bulldozer. The male EMT was tall and thin. Standing together, the pair looked like a one and a zero. A perfect ten.

Officer Driver responded to the call. He looked just as fresh and young as he had the night of the graffiti. He made an attempt at interviewing the blubbering woman, but he didn't get much. In the end, the Perfect Ten rolled her out on a gurney.

Driver chewed bubble gum while he spoke to Talia and me in that vibrating baritone of his. "Who found her?" he asked around his wad of pink.

I half-raised my hand. "I did."

Talia added, "I let the poor dear in to use the restroom and ended up forgetting about her."

Driver gave Talia a steely glare.

I said, "Talia was busy trying to cheer me up. As you already know, I have a lot going on. We got to talking, and that was that."

Talia nodded. "I left the front doors open so she could get out, but I have no idea why she couldn't get out of the restroom."

Driver asked, "She say that? That she couldn't get out?"

"Yep," I told him.

Talia shook her head. "There are no locks on the doors. It's a multi-person restroom. Now, I can see someone playing a prank and locking the stalls from the inside, but there's no reason why she couldn't get out of the restroom door. I think she's loopy, the poor dear."

"Drugs, probably," Driver said. "While I was trying to ask her questions, I could see how dilated her eyes were. Maybe meth or something. Who knows? That stuff clogs you up, too, so that could account for the sheer volume of… *stuff* that finally came out of her."

I wrinkled my nose and took a step back.

Driver apologized.

I felt no need to tell Driver the other possible reasons the woman's eyes were so dilated. Fear was a good one. That emotion can also make someone unclog their bowels in a hurry. As far as the volume of *stuff* was concerned, I didn't bother trying to figure out why the woman in the Ravens jersey had been so full of it.

"You heard from Sherwood about your caller, Ella?" Driver asked.

"Not yet. Why? You got something?"

"No. The whole thing has piqued my interest, though. We haven't had much going on around town, so I've been rolling through neighborhoods, talking to people. Strikes me funny that someone waited until *after* Dane was executed before starting the harassment. Things like that get me thinking."

Talia broke in. "I'm going to excuse myself, you two. I have a rather… nasty mess to clean up."

I said, "I'll help when I'm done talking to Officer Driver."

"No need, deary. You've been through enough already. I'm a big girl. Might could stomach it better than you right now." Talia tried to laugh, but the sound died in her throat. I saw it bobbing there, in her neck, but nothing came of it.

When she'd gone, I walked with Driver to the front of the library. I asked, "What are you thinking so hard about? I thought you were of the same opinion that Sherwood was. Just some fool kids."

"Seems to be the popular consensus, really, it does, even around the station, but something doesn't fit right. Like I said before, why'd they wait until after Dane's death? You have any guesses?"

"I wasn't home is one. During the trials, I spent my entire life savings, along with my husband's death benefits. I even took out a new mortgage, trying to run around God's green earth and be there for Dane. I was a fool. I know that now."

"No. You're a mother. I don't know what I'd do in your shoes should I ever find out my daughter's capable of evil... I-I'm sorry." Driver stopped and put his hand out as if he wanted to touch my forearm, but he never made contact. "That was uncalled for."

"I know what you meant." I let out a long sigh. "Dane *was* evil, so I can't argue with you about *that*. But you're right. I'm his mother... *was* his mother. Everyone seems to forget the connection that implies."

"True. Too true. So did you find anything out of place or disturbed when you finally got back home? Any sign that someone had been around the house?"

"Not that stood out. I guess anyone could have been by and I wouldn't have had a clue. I don't speak to my neighbors. I think they would like to keep it that way."

"Any of your neighbors ever say anything to you about Dane?"

"No. I'm just assuming."

Driver offered another sheepish smile. He looked ten years younger every time he did. "How are you holding up? Been sleeping?"

His questioning took me aback. All of a sudden, he was talking to me as if we were old chums who hadn't seen each other in years. I answered politely, "Sleep? What's that?"

He laughed, and it seemed genuine. "I can understand that."

"You say you have a daughter?" I figured I'd play along with his getting-to-know-me routine.

"Helena. She's four."

"And I'm betting she's spoiled rotten."

"We do our best."

"Daddy's girl?"

Driver waved a hand. "Oh no, definitely not. She's latched onto her mother with superglue most days."

"She'll come around. I didn't like my father none too much until I was a teenager."

Driver blushed. His stubble looked like a bunch of dead trees in a blood-colored swamp. "Yeah. That's what everyone tells me. That and she'll start rotating her head and spitting pea soup when she hits puberty. I'm *so* looking forward to that one."

We stepped out into the dying light of the day. I was shocked I couldn't find the sun in the sky. "What time is it?"

Driver pulled a cell phone from his breast pocket and slid his finger across the screen to unlock it. "Almost seven. When did you find the woman in the bathroom?"

"Just after five. Sheesh, time flies when you run across someone swimming in poop."

Driver shook his head. "Yuck. The things drugs do to people, I swear."

"Yeah… drugs. Bad stuff to get into."

"Keep your ringer turned on, Ella. I might have some more questions for you if it turns out something comes of the lady in the restroom."

"What could you possibly find out? She's crazy is what I'm guessing."

"Could be. But I still can't think of a reason why she just didn't crawl under the stall doors."

I already worked that one out, Mister Policeman. But I wasn't going to voice my opinion. What was I going to tell him, that I was being haunted? I'd seen enough of the people around town whispering and sneering. It was nice to have someone other than Talia who didn't treat me as if I was the one who'd killed all those people. I shrugged. "Like you said, drugs and whatnot."

"Maybe." Driver shook my hand and left by way of the wraparound walkway.

A minute later, I saw his blue cruiser pull out of the parking lot. He waved to me, and I returned the gesture.

Back inside, I joined Talia in the ladies' room. She'd managed to mop up the entire mess while Driver and I had been talking. I was impressed and told her so.

"Not my first rodeo, Ella. My mother had Sundowners on top of her dementia. She'd get up in the middle of the night and fling her poo everywhere. Mind you, this wasn't my mother's filth, but I made do."

I flinched at the word "filth." *You sit in your filth, little boy, and you think about what you done.* Without thinking over the subject too hard, I told Talia, "I don't… I don't want to go back to my house tonight. I was talking with Officer Driver, and our conversation unsettled me." I was lying. I just didn't want to be home alone. If Dane could keep a stranger locked in a

110

bathroom, I didn't want to consider what he would be able to do to me in the privacy of my home. "With everything that's going on, I'm feeling a little… unsafe."

Talia pushed the yellow mop bucket full of foul-smelling sludge into the nearest corner and leaned the mop handle against the wall. She strode across the tile floor and put a consoling hand on my shoulder. "You can stay with me if you want."

"That's not what I meant." I laughed, pulling away gently. "I was going to ask you to loan me money for a hotel room. My check doesn't come in until tomorrow, so I'm tapped."

"Oh, I see." She actually looked defeated. It occurred to me that Talia was far lonelier than she'd ever let on.

I sighed. "If you want me to, I will. I was just saying that staying with you hadn't crossed my mind."

"Oh, good. We can have a ladies' night! Maybe do some of that drinking I've been considering, eh?" Talia winked at me.

"Why not? Could be fun. I can't remember the last time I had any of that stuff. Fun, I mean."

"It's a date, then. You might want to consider going home to change first." She pointed at the damp spot on the front of my blouse. I'd forgotten all about throwing up on myself.

Leaving Talia alone to finish the disposal of the filth in the mop bucket, I drove home. She assured me she would be fine, so I didn't argue.

My house was dark, foreboding. Even after I turned on every single light in the place, the air still felt heavy with my dread. Every corner I rounded, I expected to see Dane pop out holding a handful of teeth or childhood Dane crawling down a wall toward me.

111

As I progressed, I whispered, "Yea, though I walk through the valley of the shadow of death…"

I considered the possibility that I had already lost my mind, that Dane was nothing more than my own mental conjuring, that Doc Morrow was a figment of my imagination as well as Melissa and the DVD and Sven Gödel and the painters and the writing on my wall. What proof did I have that anyone or anything actually existed? What proof did anyone have? Madness was a slippery slope, and I had butter for shoes.

I changed in my bedroom. Shadows thrown from the ceiling fan caused me to start more than once. I was sure, many times, that Dane was right behind me, waiting. I checked the mirror above my dresser because, somehow, I felt turning around would prove dangerous. I put my dirty blouse in a plastic grocery bag, intent on washing it when I got to Talia's house. Slinging the tied-off sack over my shoulder, like a hobo ready for the rails, I jogged down the hallway to the front door. I left all the lights in the house shining brightly, locked the front door, and jogged down the steps to the driveway where my Camry awaited.

Talia lived in a double-wide trailer on Rural Route 6. The home sat back off the highway a good hundred feet and could be accessed only by a rain-rutted dirt road. My car shook and shimmied as I approached her abode. The porch's bug light was on, lending an orange glow to the space under the tin roof. Talia sat in that drab light, drinking from a glass that held a pale, pink fluid.

She waved as I got out of the car. "I didn't expect you to be here so quick. I was just letting the day wear off my bones." She stood when I got to the steps of the porch. "Can I get you a cocktail?"

"A big one, please." The lack of Dane was getting to me. Sure, I had seen him earlier sitting on that commode in the ladies' room, but I'd convinced myself he had at least one more showing left in him.

"Sit down. I'll mix you something proper." She pulled open her screen door and disappeared inside the trailer.

Three rocking chairs sat in a line to the left of the front door. The one she'd been using rocked back and forth lazily, the boards under it creaking. I headed for the adjacent chair, then saw the woman in the Ravens jersey propped up against the wall of Talia's trailer. She was reaching for me with her brown hands.

"Baaaaaaaah!" I didn't know why sheep sounds came from me, but they did. The woman disappeared, though. I supposed my gibberish scared her off.

The line between the real and unreal was continuing to blur for me. I knew the jersey-clad blond woman hadn't been there, but the thought of her hiding in my subconscious disturbed me greatly. I had almost become accustomed to shaking like a patient with Parkinson's. I stared at my twitching digits, praying the fear would pass. The woman in the Ravens jersey wasn't dead, so unlike Dane, she was no ghost. My brain was dragging me through the wringer. Alcohol was definitely in order.

Talia came back outside with a tumbler three-fingers full of the same pink beverage she was drinking. She handed me the glass, and I smelled it. The aroma pleased me.

"What *is* this?" I asked.

"It's a recipe I found online: passion fruit, pink grapefruit juice, and citrus flavored vodka. The end, I tell you. We'll be stumbling inside before we realize our teeth are swimming."

Teeth? Why did she have to use *teeth* in her metaphor?

I took a sip before sitting down. The stuff tasted even better than it smelled. I hated to ruin the flavor of the drink, but my nerves were on edge, and I'd never been able to enjoy alcohol without smoking. I reached into my purse, pulled out my pack and lighter, then fired up. The smoke felt good in the back of my throat, just that right amount of burn. I took another drink and quelled the fire. I sat down and settled in to enjoy Talia's company.

"You think that poor dear was really on drugs?" Talia asked as she took her own seat again.

The tin roof overhead popped. A section at the left end dipped down a good two inches before springing back up.

I tried to ignore it. "No other explanation. Well, I guess mental illness could be the culprit."

"Sad state of affairs, either way." Talia sipped her drink. "I do hope she'll be all right. She looked horrified."

I chuckled. "And we didn't?"

The tin roof sank again, deeper, as if more weight had been applied the second time. Talia didn't mention it, so neither did I.

Talia took a drink, licked her lips, then asked, "Can I be candid with you, Ella?"

"Are you going to suggest I get laid again?"

"No. Not yet," she said with a wink. "But I would like to know about Phil."

"What about Phil?"

The roof went *crrrrrrrrrrrrrrrrk, pop*! and I jumped.

Talia didn't seem to notice. She stared into her glass, lost in thought. "Was Phil a good man? I mean, I can't seem to find a gentleman in the lot of them. I've searched high and low" — *crrrrrrrrrrrrrrrrk, pop*! — "at church and in the classifieds, and I" — *crrrrrrrrrrrrrrrrk, pop*! — "can't seem to find anyone."

I tried to pay attention to Talia, but I was failing horribly. My head throbbed until I felt as if my skull would split open.

Crrrrrrrrrrrrrrrrk, pop! The indentation was right above my head. I didn't want to think about it, but I couldn't help it. Someone was up there walking across the roof. And he was heavy.

"Ella?"

"Yes!" I screamed.

Talia had been leaning forward, seemingly intent on tapping me upon the knee, but at my outburst, she flung herself back, almost overturning her chair in the process. Her drink landed in her lap. "Hooey, that's cold!" She leapt out of her chair and shook ice out from her skirt. The tumbler hit the wood of the porch with a dull thump, but I barely heard it over —

Crrrrrrrrrrrrrrrrk, pop!

— the noise on the roof.

Talia continued to swipe liquid off her dress, but managed to say, "Are… are you all right?"

"Yeah, I… uh… I thought I saw a spider."

She looked at me queerly. "But you screamed 'yes.'"

"You… you caught me off guard is all."

"I have to change." Talia pulled open the screen door and stepped inside her trailer. She called out, "Be right back!"

Talia's glass spun in oblong patterns across the porch until it came to the stoop and dropped out of sight onto the first step. I heard the tumbler descend the stairs, one thump at a time.

Two prison-issue sandals dropped down over the edge of the roof, a pair of orange legs attached to them. I saw them, but the sight didn't register right away. What I actually thought I saw in that moment was Fredericka Devereau's pink sneakers and plaid Capri pants.

I began backing away, my heart drumming *Wipeout* against my ribcage. The legs kicked slowly, like a lazy child on a swing. I screamed.

Dane's face appeared inch by terrible inch. He rested his chin on the edge of the roof and smiled. "Hey, Momma."

I tore open Talia's screen door and ran inside the trailer. Stumbling on the kick plate, I went down to my knees on the floor of the foyer.

Behind me, Dane called, "Mommmmm-ahhhhh."

I used the knob of the front door as leverage and pulled myself up. I could feel Dane breathing down my neck. I heard the roof—

Crrrrrrrrrrrrrrrrk, pop!

—and it made me move faster.

Though I wasn't familiar with Talia's trailer, I had no trouble navigating my way as I plunged deeper into her house. I passed through an open-faced kitchen and into a narrow, unlit hallway. I slapped the walls on each side, trying to find a light switch, not wanting to take the corridor in the diffuse light coming from the kitchen.

My mind screamed, "Where's the damn switch?" I had no intention of looking back, but I did all the same.

In the middle of the living room, Dane was hunkered down in a catcher's stance, cracking his knuckles and laughing. Not an ounce of mirth could be found in the sound.

I whipped my head back around, not wanting to see him anymore. "God, don't let this be real. Please, *Lord*, please, let me be dreaming."

Garth Brooks was wrong. God's greatest gifts were definitely *not* unanswered prayers. I shouted, "Talia!"

I ran past a closed door on the right, but heard it creaking open behind me. Throwing myself into a wall on my left, I chanced a glance back at the living room.

Dane had vanished.

The hallway filled with sudden bright light. I squinted against the startling illumination and shielded my eyes.

Wicked thumps and crunching noises came from the room I had passed. I heard moans, tired-sounding and soul-killing. I hugged the wall. Sliding down the hall about a foot at a time, I came to the open door—a small bathroom.

Talia, bent at the waist, was naked in front of her sink. Her skirt and blouse lay in a pile on the floor in front of the bathtub. Blood dripped from the lip of the sink, plinking onto the linoleum.

Dane backed out of Talia as if he were simply passing through an archway into the regular world. He reached out to the back of Talia's head with one hand, his fingers entwined in her long brown hair. He tugged, and Talia shot bolt upright. Her mouth was a grotesque parody of skin and teeth.

She turned her head and glared at me with dead eyes. "Hellllll eeeeee."

Dane shoved her face back onto the edge of the sink.

117

One of Talia's legs kicked backward, put a hole in the wall behind her, and went rigid. Dane laughed. The noise sounded of the grave.

Again, he pulled up Talia's head. Bloody teeth fell from her mouth and clicked against the tiled floor. Her eyes rolled back in her head, and her arms went limp. Dane released her hair, and she collapsed, a motionless lump next to her pile of clothes.

He knelt and picked up a tooth. He seemed distracted, so enamored by the tooth that he'd forgotten I was even there. Finally, he said, "Feels good to be back, Momma. You felt this coming, didn't you?"

I unglued myself from my position against the wall and bolted to the front door. Ripping it open, I ran outside, shrieking like a banshee in the night. Down the porch steps I went, and my foot found Talia's discarded tumbler.

I flew through the air with the greatest of ease. I landed on my chest, and all the wind in the world left my general vicinity. Breath became acidic. The blood in my veins turned into nuclear waste. I rolled from side to side, clutching my chest, praying to God for the entirety of life to end.

Dane no longer resided in Talia's bathroom. He presided over my thoughts.

"I can do so much now, Momma. Your baby boy's almost home. Too bad Daddy's gonna miss the festivities."

I managed to push myself up to my knees. I crawled to the Camry. Using the fender, I got to my feet. Still struggling to catch my breath, I dug around in my pants for the car keys, latched onto them, and opened the car door with my free hand. I poured myself into the driver's seat.

It took me several minutes to find the ignition box. Several times, I melted down. I beat the devil out of the steering wheel with the balls of my fists, screaming words I'd never uttered, calling my dashboard all kinds of promiscuous, unclean women and likening it to those fond of fellatio.

Dane's voice hummed in my mind. "Run, Momma. Don't you look back neither. You run and go see my Melissa. Run now."

I was surprised I didn't snap an axle backing down that rutted road. I left Talia's trailer in a plume of reddish-brown dust. The Camry swung into the road in reverse. I took one final look back at the trailer.

In the glow of the bug light, I could see Talia standing on the first step of the front porch. Dane had an arm around her, keeping her corpse upright. He lifted one of her arms and made Talia wave at me.

I heard Dane, crystal clear, from a hundred feet away. "See you soon."

SIXTEEN

AFTER DANE THREW PHIL THROUGH our sliding glass door, life got better. I couldn't help but think that if Dane had reacted earlier, our lives might have been less complicated. There I was, inactive and scared, unable to help my child out of fear for my own safety. Seeing Phil as a defeated bully gave me a bit of joy. The time had been long coming, so I settled in and worshipped it.

One morning, months after Dane's departure, Phil sat across the dining room table from me, eating a bowl of high-fiber cereal. Even with a closed mouth, he chewed loudly. The *crunch, crunch, crunch* annoyed me. I could feel a headache starting to form, so I left my bowl of Raisin Flakes to fetch a bottle of Tylenol.

Phil grunted, a feral sound like that of an angry boar. I turned around, my hand still on the cabinet door, and saw Phil extract a piece of broken tooth from his mouth. He held it pinched between his thumb and forefinger. His tooth and fingers, covered in specks of brown cereal, dripped milk. Phil growled, "Son of a bitch."

I didn't miss a beat. "Now you know how Dane felt when you knocked *his* teeth out… *both times.*"

Before Dane left, I would never have said something like that to Phil. It felt good, that comment did. Still, I paused, that contented feeling drifting off into the ether just as soon as it had come.

Phil rose from his chair in one quick movement. He threw the table aside with a swipe of his thick arms. He took my hair in his fist, opened the fridge, and began slamming the door closed on my head.

None of that really happened, but I imagined it as clearly as if it had.

Instead of battering me by way of Frigidaire, Phil simply stared at me like a wounded animal. I asked myself, *Could this vile, vicious man actually be warring with himself over the hell he'd put Dane through?*

Phil's eyes melted and leaked down onto his cheeks. He cried for some time. I didn't count the minutes, but I was sure I could have watched an entire episode of Oprah while I stood there holding the cabinet door.

"It hurts." Phil stared at the tooth, shaking his head. "I didn't know it would hurt so much."

I thought he was talking about his mouth, so I grabbed the bottle of Tylenol, took three out for myself, then put the bottle on the table in front of my weeping husband. I sat down again and went back to my cereal.

The pills rattled as Phil pushed the bottle toward me. "I don't need it. I gotta think about what I done. Let me hurt."

I probably looked like a dull-eyed cow chewing its cud. I stared at Phil, wondering what to say, but finally settled on nothing.

Phil obviously loved his son. Why, then, had he felt the need to beat Dane and humiliate him almost constantly? People didn't torture someone they cared for, did they? Those questions and hundreds more kept me quiet. Maybe Dane returning the pain upon Phil had finally wised up my husband to the abuse he'd rained down over the years. I would never understand Phil's sudden change, so I stopped considering the possibilities.

I ate my cereal.

SEVENTEEN

TALIA WAS DEAD.

Dane had killed her.

And I'd run away from the scene of a crime.

Those thoughts kept repeating themselves, in that order, over and over in my head. I took back roads home, avoiding main thoroughfares and the Watercourse Crossway Bridge like the plague. I drove well enough not to get pulled over, but that didn't mean Dane hadn't seen fit to bust one of my taillights without me knowing. It wasn't as if I'd had the time for a twelve-point inspection before my Houdini act back at Talia's trailer.

I didn't understand much, aside from the fact that my serial-killer son had become an apparition that could do as he pleased in the real world. Dane's ushering words didn't make sense to me. In the video Sven Gödel gave me, Dane's warning to his Melissa had been clear. *Stay away from my mother.* If I was such bad news, then why was Dane pushing me in her direction? The more I tried to make sense of it, the further away my logical thoughts seemed to scamper, like school children set free for the summer.

When I pulled onto my street, my headlights found a black Mercedes parked on the street in front of my home. It seemed Sven Gödel thought another visit was on the menu that evening. I had enough on my plate without that leech coming to suckle what little blood I had left to give.

Plus, I was running from a possible murder charge. After all, who was going to believe me? My fingerprints and hair fibers and Lord knows what else had been left behind at Talia's trailer. It wouldn't be long before they found her body. The library wouldn't open as planned in the morning, and someone would investigate. They'd find Talia's crushed-in face on that bathroom floor and start asking who she'd last been seen with. Officer Driver would tell them that that someone was most definitely Ella May Peters, mother of the Rest Stop Dentist. And didn't it just fit that most of Talia's teeth had been knocked clean out of her mouth?

I'd read plenty of nonfiction crime stories in my day and had seen enough *CSI Miami* and *NCIS* to know I was going down the river, quick like a bunny. First things first, though, I had to get rid of Sven.

I parked the Camry in the driveway and got out. Sven was already coming around his own car. I didn't acknowledge him. I quickened my pace, taking long strides toward my porch steps.

"Ella!" Sven's voice sounded urgent, very unlike him.

"I don't have time for you!" I took the four steps two at a time. Shoving my key into the deadbolt, I turned it and pushed on the door.

"Ella, we need to talk!"

"Not now, Sven!"

Snick.

The sound hadn't come from my door or my entry into the house. It came from behind me. I paused, some deep section of my psyche doing the math in my head, twisting and turning the numbers until they lined up and revealed the answer to the equation.

Stomping footsteps came up my stairs. Slowly, I turned.

Sven was a mess. His disheveled blond hair hung from his scalp, covering his face in oily strands. Stubble bristled on his square jaw, a five o'clock shadow gone far past midnight. The jacket of his three-piece suit was gone, but I recognized the tie from the last time I had seen it two weeks prior. Then, it had been loose. Now, the necktie was draped across his shoulders. The tie was darkened at the tip, as if Sven had dipped it in ink. My porch light made his white shirt yellow, and the red bird on his chest orange.

I realized two things at one time.

The crimson crow on Sven's shirt was a rictus of still-damp blood. It could have been something else, but considering he was also aiming a rather large handgun at my face, I doubted it was strawberry jelly.

On instinct alone, I began backing into my home. I sounded like a terrified little girl when I said, "Wh-what are you doing?"

"You know good and well, Ella." He tilted his head, and the gun went with it. With his pistol sideways, Sven looked like a gang member from one of those gritty ghetto dramas, as if he imagined he could throw the bullets out faster that way.

I inched another step back. "I don't understand. Why?"

"Why do we do anything? Because Dane tells us to."

From less than three feet away, Sven pulled the trigger.

Quasimodo, hopped up on crank and caffeine, made bells toll in the church tower of my mind. In a flash of brilliant fire and light, I knew how tinnitus suffers felt. The ringing in my ears built to a crescendo, and I was certain my skull would explode.

When I finally became able to open my eyes — which I didn't remember shutting — black orbs swam through my vision, blocking light in wide, oblong patterns. How I got to my knees in the doorway of my home, I couldn't recall. I'd been shot, but where? I patted the front of my blouse, felt around my neck and head, then ran my fingers through my hair. My hands didn't come back sticky with blood, nor did I feel any pain.

I was unceremoniously shoved into the doorframe by Sven, who stepped inside the foyer. I twisted to my right, keeping the frame of the doorway at my back for support, and looked into the house.

My vision was beginning to return to normal, but my ears still projected amplified, discordant flute music. Jethro Tull played "Aqualung" from his place next to my eardrums. Brown, mud-caked boots were the first thing that registered. They were attached to the jean-clad legs of a prone individual. The black hoodie was unmistakable. Gone were the skeletal jaw-line bandana and black gloves with white metacarpals, but I knew it was the same person who had spray-painted my house.

I took in everything else in less than a second's time. My living room walls were covered in black lettering. Foul language was most present, calling me names fit for ladies of the night and persons who copulated with their mothers. But even with all that, one sentence stood out above all the rest: *THEY SHOULD HAVE KILLED U 2.*

The side living room window had been broken, no doubt so the person could gain entrance, being that my front door had still been locked. His twitching hand held a crowbar—possibly the object he'd used to break the glass. I could see his knuckles whitening and darkening, the tendons in the back of his hand flexing as he tried to keep hold of the heavy tool.

Sven stepped forward and kicked the crowbar from the man's hand. It flopped, end over end, and landed with a clang in the kitchen. I managed to get up, pushing with my palms on my knees for support as I rose. Having a higher view than before, I was able to see the gunshot wound in the neck and the bloody bandage wrapped around the left wrist. Then, it hit me. He'd stabbed his hand opening a paint can.

"Stanley?" Actually, I wasn't a bit shocked—confused, yes, but not surprised in the least. I'd never done anything to the man. Still, I could see him leaning in to warn Frank that day they'd arrived to cover up the graffiti, perhaps to say, "Watch it. She's that serial killer's momma." How ironic was it that I'd called the company he worked for to fix the mess Stanley, himself, had made?

The bullet had hit Stanley in the dead center of his neck. Where his Adam's apple should have been, there was nothing but bubbling blood. Every time he tried to breathe in, the hole in his neck would wheeze, allowing his oxygen to escape back into the world. He wouldn't be among us for long.

My voice calm and sure, I asked Sven, "Why'd you shoot him?"

"He was coming at you with the crowbar." Sven's deadpan delivery was garbled, as if spoken from underwater. I was sure my ringing ears were to blame.

129

Questions overcame me, so I let them rip all at once. "Why do you even have a gun? Why are you bloody? Why are you in the same clothes you were in two weeks ago?" My tone ascended after each one until I yelled the last of my questions.

"Long story. He's dead. We gotta go." Sven grabbed my arm and dragged me out onto the porch.

"I don't want to go anywhere with you," I said, as if that would stop a madman with a miniature cannon in his fist. I tried to tear myself away from him, but his strength far exceeded mine. Nails dug into the soft flesh of my forearm the more I struggled, so I finally just followed him.

"You don't have a choice. This gun is loud. People will have called the cops."

Talia's smashed face flitted into my mind. If I got reeled in by the local police, I wouldn't have an ice cube's chance in hell of finding out why Dane was playing his games.

Sven opened the passenger side door of his Mercedes with his gun hand, using his pinkie and ring finger to lift the handle, and swung me inside with his other hand. I settled onto the leather seat. When Sven slammed the door, my ears popped something fierce-like, and I imagined my brain had collapsed in on itself. I covered my ears, even though I knew the noise was coming from inside my own head, and willed the dissonance to stop.

A moment later, Sven dropped into the driver's seat. He started the car, then rolled down his window. My ears popped again, and I screeched like a mouse in a trap. That pop settled the hunchback that ran rampant in my head. I could hear Sven clearly the next time he spoke.

"We're leaving town. Dane wants us to see his Melissa. I intend on finding out what's going on. If you want, I'll drop you off somewhere. He'll kill you, though. Make no mistake about that. I tried to resist, and well…" Sven looked down at his chest, to the red bird there. "Now look at me." He put the car into gear and pulled away from the curb.

"So you've seen Dane, too?" I asked.

"More than just *seen* him."

I shook my head, confused. "What do you have to do with any of this? What's he got against you?"

"I guess he didn't like my style of journalism." Sven stopped at the end of the street, put on his right turn signal, then met my eyes. "Everyone's a critic, huh?"

I didn't hear any sirens, though I was sure they would come eventually. Sven drove us through quiet, sleeping neighborhoods, using a GPS app with some faint British accent to guide him. The voice came from a smart phone Sven had attached to a clasp on the dash. Technology never ceased to amaze me. The Brit on the phone told Sven to make a right, and he turned in the direction of the interstate.

I asked, "You think the highway is a good idea?"

"We're in a hurry. Don't have much of a choice."

I sighed and settled back into the seat.

Sven said, "The controls for the seat are down on the side by the door. Even a heater."

"I'm not cold."

"You will be. Dane shows up, and you'll be freezing."

"I haven't noticed any difference when he pops up."

Sven glanced at me curiously. "Strange."

Houses became more sparse until they disappeared altogether. The woods ended at a highway ramp. At some point, the road hypnotized me, the broken white lines on the pavement lulling me into a trance-like state.

Clearing his throat, Sven asked, "How long has Dane been showing up for you?"

"Since he died. The first time I saw him was the night of his funeral. He… played with me while I was grocery shopping."

"Was anyone around?" Sven put on his turn signal, though there were no other cars on the road, and entered the fast lane. The speedometer hit eighty before he turned on the cruise control.

"No one of importance. He popped up again a couple of days later at my house. My friend Talia was there. She's dead now. Dane killed her." I filled him in on the happenings at Talia's trailer.

He kept nodding while I related the recent events as if they were the most commonplace occurrences he'd ever heard. I wanted to know his story, but I also had a need to tell my own. I needed to spill my guts, to get it out. The floodgates opened, and I turned into a blubbering mess as I recounted Talia's horrid end.

Sven reached into the center console and pulled out a travel pack of Kleenex. He offered me one. I blew my nose with it, crumbled it up, and dropped it into the console. With a grimace, Sven snatched up my damp tissue. He rolled down his window and threw out the soggy paper.

I asked, "You think littering is a good idea?"

"Sorry, but that's the least of our worries."

"We get pulled over because a state trooper sees you tossing stuff out your window, and we'll have plenty to worry about."

"Good point." He rolled up his window. "So this Talia, she was around when you first saw Dane?"

"No. Only the cashier and some other employee. Those two didn't have anything to do with Dane if that's what you're thinking."

"No, that's not what I was thinking. I'm a fan of those ghost-hunting reality shows."

I laughed. I couldn't help myself. I had never been able to stomach those foolish things. But my laughter died when I realized I was pretty much living one of those shows at that moment. "Sorry. Go on," I said.

"No worries. I never lent them much credence myself, before Dane. They were… entertainment, I guess. But now that I look back on all that nonsense, I'm starting to come to terms with a few facts."

"Like?"

"Ghosts, for lack of a better, less idiotic word, draw energy from people. The more people, the more energy. The more energy, the more power the ghost has to… do things."

I nodded, though I didn't fully agree with him. Dane had shown up to mess with me plenty of times while no one was around. Then again, *I* had been there, so Sven's theory wasn't completely insane.

Sven asked, "You've *never* felt cold spots?"

"Not that I'm aware of. But when Dane pops up, I don't actually check the thermometer, if you know what I mean."

"Fair enough. Well, I feel them. Maybe I'm more sensitive. I am a bit worse-for-wear than you are." Sven looked down at the red bird on his chest and shuddered.

"What the heck happened to you anyway? You reek something fierce." Since I'd been in the car with him for a while, his body odor was becoming quite repugnant.

"I'm assuming you haven't changed or showered since you brought me that video."

He nodded. His confessing to his lack of hygiene seemed to make his funk worse. I crinkled my nose and turned my head, looking out the window at the guardrails and concrete barriers that framed the interstate.

Sven said, "I don't give up this information lightly, as it disrupts my pride, but maybe you'll glean some information from it. He… won't let me change clothes. Won't let me get anywhere near water. I got my coat off only because he pulled it off while I was trying to run away. Other than that, I'm stuck. My buttons won't come undone. My zipper's not moving. I'm… I'm not in a good place."

"You can say that again." A thought occurred to me. "How are you going to the bathroom?"

"He lets me do that much. But as soon as I'm done, he dresses me again."

"My Dane always was a considerate kid."

Sven found that all too funny. His head snapped back, and he burst into guffaws. I did not share in his mirth.

Sven's laughter calmed, and he said, "Dane killed the maid at my hotel this afternoon. I woke up with her facedown on my shirt."

I felt a shiver run down my spine.

He continued, "I'm only guessing here, but I figure she came in to check to see if I needed my room cleaned. I had been unable to leave the room, so I couldn't put the Do Not Disturb sign on the handle. I assume Dane got to her, snatched all the teeth from her head, and laid her on me while I slept."

"Management never checked on you? Didn't you have to pay for your extra days?"

"Credit card was on file. I do that no matter where I check in because I never know how much of my time a story will take up. My publication foots the bill."

"So you haven't left your hotel room for two weeks?"

Sven nodded. "I even tried to call my boyfriend, Brandon, but my phone always goes dead before the call will go through. The hotel room's phone wouldn't even give me a dial tone." Sven took his eyes off the road and judged the surprise on my face with a wan smile. "No worries, Christian Lady, I'm only half a fag."

"That's a *vile* thing to call yourself. And I'm quite sure it's none of my business." I averted my eyes. The Old Testament taught that homosexuality was a sin in the eyes of the Lord, but it wasn't my place to say so. Sven would see the error in his ways, or he would see Hell. He didn't need me preaching to him. I focused on the road, on the sea of gray being swept up under the Mercedes.

"I'm *bi*-sexual. Brandon is just my *soup du jour*."

A black sedan sped past. I hadn't even seen the approach of the headlights. That car must've been going a hundred if it was going ten. I told him, "I am not God, Sven. Judgment is *His* job."

"Fair enough. Thank you for calling me Sven, by the way. That 'Mr. Gödel' nonsense was beginning to irk me."

The whole *bi-thing* had gotten under my skin more than I wanted to admit, but Sven's last comment served as the straw that broke the camel's back. "You know what irks *me*, Mr. Gödel?"

He sighed. "Here we go."

"You're right, 'here we go'... *again*. You publicized and glorified the death of my son. And after he died, you made me look like a fool. Like an ignorant mother who just turned her head to her son's actions. I never told you because it was none of your gosh-darn business, but I didn't know what Dane was doing, nor did I condone it. But you didn't *know* that, so you assumed. *That*, Mr. Gödel, irked me something fierce. So pardon me if you're *irked* by me calling you 'Mr. Gödel,' *Mr. Gödel!*" When I ceased my diatribe, I realized I'd cut into the leather of Sven's passenger seat with my nails, I'd been grabbing it so hard. I released the pressure, and my knuckles creaked with relief.

"I suppose I deserved that outburst."

"You're lucky that's all you got. I swear, your nerve. I feel sick just riding in the same car with you, you know that?"

"My, my, I do bother you, don't I? A woman of your charm reaching down to her depths to drag out a comment like that, just... wow. I'm floored."

"What can I say? You bring out the best in me."

Sven grew silent. I figured he was mulling over just what he had done to me during the course of Dane's trial and, finally, after Dane's death. I wanted to remain angry, to keep that burning hatred for Sven Gödel, but as I sat there, I could feel it ebbing away like sea foam being dragged back to the ocean on the tide.

Sven was not my enemy. He was a vile, putrid, money-hungry journalist for sure, but not my enemy. Not anymore. I didn't even know if I could label Dane my enemy. Dane was still my son. I had to keep telling myself that.

Sven broke the silence after — according to the clock on the cell phone that hung from the dash — ten minutes. "Dane told me you were in trouble. Said someone was going to try and hurt you. He wants us alive… for now."

"I'm not going to try and make sense of any of this. I'm done with that." I shook my head. "He'll do what he wants. I have no doubt about that."

"I don't know anything, either. I'm just glad I had my gun with me on this trip. Sometimes I keep it at home, but I had to drive through Kansas to get to you, and those boys can get serious about rainbow bumper stickers. There's one on the rear of the car, in case you didn't notice."

"Never did."

"I've been accosted more than once for my… sexual preference. I bought the gun as a protective measure. I bet you're glad I did, huh?"

"I'm never glad to see someone killed, Sven."

"Back to Sven again, I see."

"For now."

"I'm glad. We're in this together whether you're okay with it or not."

"Oh, trust me… I get that. I may not like it, but I get *that* better than anything. At least I'm not alone." I wrapped my arms around myself and massaged my biceps. Gooseflesh rose, making the fine hair on my forearms stand up. "Can you turn on the heat?"

Sven looked into the rearview mirror, and his eyes glowed green from the dashboard lights. "Won't make a difference. Dane's in the back seat. He's been there for a while now."

I have no idea what version of Dane that Sven saw, but I heard Child Dane's voice. "Don't mind me, Momma. I'm just enjoying the ride."

Dane always did like to travel.

EIGHTEEN

PHIL BOUGHT A WINNEBAGO THREE days before Dane turned ten. The recreational vehicle stood tall at over fifteen feet and long as all get out at forty feet. The sides rolled out into tents, and beds could be placed in the bay-window-styled sections. The kitchen was immense, with a working sink and a faux wood countertop, an island for food preparation, and burners that ran off a propane tank hidden under the sink. The one bathroom was huge, plenty of room for Phil and me to be in there at the same time. The toilet was state of the art, instead of the old-fashioned chemical type, and burned refuse in a controlled incinerator. The driver's and passenger's seats were La-Z-Boy branded. They molded to my rump, hugged and protected it. Riding in that RV was like floating on a cloud in heaven.

Phil said the RV wasn't all that expensive and that our bank had given him a pretty low APR on the loan he'd taken out to purchase it. I didn't question him. He rarely did anything nice for the family, so I wasn't going to look a gift horse in the mouth. Phil buying that rolling house was one of the good times I fell back on when things got too bad. Maybe that was why he did it. That RV might've been the proverbial carrot dangled before a horse.

I, of course, didn't know what Phil had planned, so I'd gotten Dane a different sort of birthday present. Dane never had many friends growing up, so I figured I'd get him something living to play with. I rescued a solid white cat from the kill shelter in Denver just one week before the poor thing was set to be euthanized. She was an older cat, six years by the shelter's guesstimate, and had a pink nose that always seemed warm and moist, which surprised me. All the cats I owned growing up—and there were a plethora of them—had cold noses, so I just assumed all felines did. Dane named her Bear, for whatever reason. Phil accepted her well enough, even after he found out I'd spent over a hundred dollars in pound fees and the necessities that came with owning a cat, like food, kitty litter, and toys.

Because Bear had been a sudden, unexpected addition to our family, quite like the RV, we had no time to find someone to watch the new cat. So Bear came with us on our very first family vacation.

Before we even left our driveway, Phil gave Dane one instruction regarding Bear. "You be mindful of it. Your mother spent a whole lotta money on that animal."

Smiling, Dane nodded with fervor.

Our ascent into the Rocky Mountains took nine hours, mainly because we were constantly waylaid by restroom needs. Dane's bladder seemed to shrink in the higher elevation. Fifteen rest areas later, we arrived at our destination.

Phil told me an engineer friend of his had given him the location. Phil said campgrounds weren't *real* camping; too many people and amenities spoiled the "roughing it" aspect. I thought about the lavish rolling abode Phil had purchased for the trip, the irony not lost on me, and giggled inwardly.

Phil pulled the RV onto a secluded dirt road lined with trees and scrub brush. It was mid-October, but snow covered everything at that altitude. I watched the miles tick up to seven and a half before Phil turned onto a flat section on the right that reminded me of the pet cemetery in that one movie, but without the rock circles.

Phil set the parking brake and twisted in his seat to look at me. "Whataya think?"

I said, "It's out of the way; that's for sure. I'm glad I packed enough food for a month should we get stuck out here."

"Ain't nothing gonna happen." Phil waved a hand in dismissal. "Chuck says we won't be bothered."

"I believe him."

"Maybe that boy of ours will learn something 'bout being a man out here. One can only hope."

"He's fine."

"Buying him a damn cat ain't helping none." Phil craned his neck to look in the back.

I followed suit. Dane sat in the kitchen area, still strapped in and petting Bear, who purred loudly from her place on the table in front of him.

Phil asked, "Why didn't you buy him a dog?"

"Dogs were twice as much."

"Blah. Shoulda bought him a dog."

I left our conversation at that.

That evening, Phil dug a hole about twenty feet from the RV with a collapsible Army-issue spade he'd brought along. I didn't know where the starter log had come from, but Phil pulled it out of the cabinet under the sink. He placed the fire brick in the hole he'd dug and lit it with a long grill lighter. Then, he added extra pine straw and fallen branches to the mix. I sat in a foldaway chair and watched the ice and snow melt off the detritus Phil had placed in the blaze.

The three of us sat around the fire that night, making s'mores and chatting. Bear was left to herself in the camper. Phil even tousled Dane's hair once or twice. When he did, though, Dane would flinch, and Phil would laugh.

The second time it happened, Phil said, "Whatcha so scared for? You ain't done nothin' to catch a beating. Enjoy yourself, boy."

It was bad that Phil had to let his son know when it was all right to relax. I tried not to focus too hard on that fact, but it still played through my mind. I didn't get to see my men like that often, so I enjoyed it.

Dane excused himself some time later. He ran inside, holding himself like boys do when their bladders refuse to hold anymore fluid, and slammed the door behind him.

While Dane was inside, I told Phil, "Thank you for this."

"Weren't nothing. I suppose I owe the boy some free time. I've been kinda hard on him as of late. But you see him? He's growing into a man, Ella. Our boy, ten going on twenty." Phil laughed. I liked the sound of it.

"Why are you so" — I chose my words carefully — "hard on him?"

Phil waved me off. "Ain't nothing my father didn't do to me. And I turned out just fine."

That could be argued, but I simply nodded.

"A boy grows into a pussy" — I grimaced at the expletive, but Phil didn't seem to notice — "if he thinks there's no violence to be had in the world. Me whuppin' on Dane is teaching him that you gotta act when someone pisses you off. It's the way of the world, Ella. You want our boy to grow up soft like you?"

I didn't answer that. Phil's words upset me, but I knew when to keep my mouth shut, for fear he'd swell it shut for me.

"A man's gotta be violent, or he welcomes violence on him. I'm not going to sit around and watch while my son gets run over for the rest of his life."

When Dane came back to the fire, he was crying. I wanted to move in on him, hug him, and ask what was wrong, but Phil beat me to the punch.

"What's the matter with you?"

Dane sniffled. "B-B-Bear's run away."

"What?" Phil and I asked in unison, only Phil's voice was much gruffer than mine.

"Please don't be mad. But I had to go real bad, a-a-and…" Dane began stammering because Phil was up out of his chair and approaching him like a stalking lion fit to kill.

Dane finally said what he was trying to say in a shotgun blast of words. "And she ran out when I opened the door!" He tucked in on himself and covered up like a boxer seeing a haymaker coming.

But Phil didn't hit the boy. Instead, he started growling. I didn't know which was worse: the possible imminent beatdown or that low, feral sound coming from Phil's diaphragm.

Phil snapped his head around to look at me. "*You* bought the cat! *You* deal with him." My husband crunched through the snow and went inside.

I was upset with Dane, but the boy was beating himself up worse than I ever could. He whimpered when I hugged him to my chest.

I petted his hair and tried to calm him. "She'll be back. She'll get hungry, Dane, and she'll come back."

Dane cried into my coat, soaking the front. When he pulled away, I had a dark smiley face staring up at me from the front of my jacket.

"She will? You think she will?"

"When you get hungry, don't you come find me and tell me?"

"Yuh-yeah."

"Well, Bear will do the same for you."

Not knowing if Phil would return, I went ahead and dropped a couple handfuls of snow onto the fire to put out the blaze. I enjoyed the smell of the smoke that poured off it. Dane cut his hand through the white plume, with a few "Ah-yahs!" for fun, like a kung fu artist chopping at his opponent's neck.

Dane and I went inside, and I set his bed up in the rollaway section just past the kitchen. I kissed him on the forehead and told him good night. When I walked back out into the narrow hall, I glanced toward the driver's cab. Phil was lurking there, playing with something on the dash.

He turned around and met my eyes. "It's plenty hot in here. I'm killing the engine for a while. Conserve gas that way." He didn't sound upset anymore.

I went left into our bedroom section without responding. He followed me a moment later. I lay down on my back in the window bed and pulled the covers up to my chest.

Phil crawled in next to me. "Cat's gone, you know. We ain't had the thing long enough for it to come back."

"It's an older cat, Phil. Plus, it's only known an inside life. The shelter told me that. It'll be back."

Phil rolled over, putting his back to me. "Or it'll freeze to death. One of them options, anyway."

Can't you just be optimistic every once in a while, you big oaf? Then, I closed my eyes and drifted off.

At some point, Phil got up and turned the heat back on. The rumbling of the engine stirred me, and I sat up in the dark. Screaming banshees faded from my dreams. I couldn't remember having a nightmare, but the sounds accompanied me out of my sleep nonetheless.

Phil came in, grumbled about being cold, and lay back down. I got back to sleep myself with little trouble.

And woke up to a different kind of screaming altogether.

Phil beat me to the door of the RV. For a man who felt the need to abuse the fire out of his only child, hearing Dane wailing like that sure made Phil move like lightning.

Phil stumbled down the two metal stairs of the RV and landed face first in the snow, cussing Satan out of Hell. I didn't pause to help him. He'd be all right, or he wouldn't. My son beckoned, and I had not one notion of stopping.

Dane knelt at the front of the RV, clutching what resembled a large rabbit's foot to his chest. The fur was matted pink. A red stick jutted from one end, looking far too much like bloodied bone. The snow around the front of the RV was speckled in red crystals. Pieces of Bear lay everywhere, all around, frozen stiff. The blood-caked fur stood in points like an angry porcupine's hide. My breath caught in my throat. I couldn't even reach for Dane. Like the dismembered cat in front of me, I was frozen in place.

Dane looked at me, sobbing. "Wha-what happened?"

In a split second, I saw what had killed of poor Bear. The fan blade.

I could see, very clearly, Phil turning off the heat the night before, then him getting up hours later to turn it back on. I heard those dreamlike banshees lamenting again.

The cat had crawled into the engine to keep warm. When Phil started the RV, she'd been hacked to pieces.

Several crazy thoughts bounded around inside my head. Had Phil done it on purpose? Even if the idea was kind of crazy, he hadn't wanted the cat, so I supposed it was possible. But was my husband capable of such things?

Phil pulled a magic trick, appearing out of nowhere, and raced toward Dane—a rampaging rhino fit to impale. Dane squeaked like a mouse caught red-handed in a trap laden with cheese and dropped the cat leg. Phil snatched the boy up by the front of his shirt, reared back, and punched him dead in the mouth. Dane's lips spurted blood. Fresh crimson joined the fading pink crystals in the snow.

Phil roared, "I told you to mind that *goddamned* cat! Didn't I, boy?"

He punched Dane again, splitting the boy's bottom lip. "You ungrateful, spoiled little brat!"

And again, Phil's fist flew. "A hundred bucks… just damn wasted!"

Dane swallowed three of his upper front teeth that day.

I just watched and prayed.

NINETEEN

SVEN DROVE US OUT OF Colorado doing ninety-five. He kept bumping up the speed, and I didn't protest. Sure, we were chancing a run-in with law enforcement, but Virginia beckoned. At one point, I mentioned that I'd left Melissa's contact info on the fridge back at my place. Sven assured me he hadn't been stupid enough to give me the information without putting it in his phone first.

Kansas welcomed us with a sign that read: Through hardships to the stars. The motto was apt, considering I was certain to be in for plenty of hardships if I left Sven's sight. Then again, what protection did Sven offer me? None, really. If Dane saw fit, he could probably kill both of us without using up too much energy. Not for the first time, I wondered what my baby boy had planned… well, the ghostly version of him, anyway.A welcome center slash rest area was coming up, and when I saw Sven put his turn signal on and felt the car slowing, I yelled, "Don't you dare!"

"I have to pee, Ella. We could use a br—"

"A rest stop? Really, Sven? All this going on and you want to stop at a *gosh-darned* rest area?"

"Oh." I could see the realization in his glowing green eyes.

"*Exactly*. Wet yourself for all I care. Not like you could smell any worse."

"That's a low blow."

"Right. I need to watch going too low. I'm sure the stink would stop my heart."

Sven curled his lip. "I do smell a bit… off."

That got me laughing. "Off? More than just… *off* by any height of the meaning, buddy."

"I wonder, now that we're on our way, if he'd let me get cleaned up?"

"I hope so. It would be in his best interest. If someone sees you with that bloody shirt, we'll be drug into court quicker than we can say, 'But he smelled so bad!'"

"Good point." Sven checked the rearview mirror and frowned. "He's gone. You think we should find a hotel?"

"I don't know about spending the night. Plus, I'm broke."

"I've got the bill." Sven smiled. "Least I can do."

My heart sped up. "Where's my purse?"

"You didn't have one on you when I saw you at the house."

I saw my handbag then, sitting next to the chair on Talia's porch. "I left it at Talia's!" I hammered the ball of my fist against the glovebox. "Well, I guess I just made the police's job that much easier. Now they won't have to question who was there with her."

"Settle down. What's done is done. We move on. I have plenty of money. Credit cards and cash galore."

I wanted to chide Sven, rub it in that all his fortune had stemmed from writing about my son, but that wouldn't help matters. I'd been stupid in leaving my purse behind, but it wasn't like I had the time, or the mind, to think about it.

"Right." I slumped down in the leather seat and sighed. "I suppose I should thank you."

"For?"

"Paying my way."

Sven laughed. "I don't have a choice. I don't want to be alone with Dane. I'll suffer you until this is over."

"Suffer me, huh? Trust me, the feeling is mutual."

Sven pointed toward the windshield, and I followed his finger. Up ahead was a sign: Goodland, 37 miles.

Sven said, "I hope they have lodging."

"Can you hold your waterworks for another half hour?"

"I'm going to have to."

"You could always find a tree. Just no rest stops."

"Fair enough. I'll do that if I have to." Sven drifted back into the fast lane and set the cruise to seventy.

"Goodland or bust. So sayeth ye complaining bladder."

Sven chuckled. "Is that Shakespeare?"

"Nope. Peters. Ella May, to be exact."

Sven took the Commerce Road exit when we hit Goodland. He drove right past the Comfort Inn with a look of disgust on his face. I supposed it wasn't up to his standards. We came to a section with a Dairy Queen on the left and a Holiday Inn Express on the right. To my surprise, he pulled into the Dairy Queen and parked around back.

Sven threw open his door and jumped out. I didn't bother watching for him after I realized what he was doing. Soon enough, I saw the steam from his urination float over the top of the dumpster area where he'd disappeared.

Sven reappeared, but instead of getting back in, he walked around the back of the car. "Pop the trunk, would you!"

I leaned across the center console and felt around in the dark until I found the button. I pushed it. The trunk came open with a dull thump. Curiosity got the better of me, so I got out and joined Sven at the back of the car.

He was in his boxers.

He half-turned away from me. "Would you mind?"

I couldn't tell if he was blushing because his skin was glowing red from the brake lights, but I imagined he was. I turned my back to him and rolled the image of him around in my mind. Sven was well built, with tight ab muscles that led down into a V where his stomach met his pubis. His calf and thigh muscles bulged in my mind, and I felt an ache that hadn't visited me in a very long time. I thought about what Talia had said about me needing to get laid. I wondered what the hell was wrong with me. I gave my mind to God, hoping He would usher away my unclean thoughts.

My imagination drifted to another scene: Talia in her bathroom, bloody face and teeth raining onto the tile at her feet. I shuddered.

I asked Sven, "Couldn't you do that when we get to the hotel?"

"And what? Check in with a bloodstained shirt? I don't think so, Ella."

I mentally kicked myself for that stupid comment. The vision of partially-nude Sven and dead Talia had scrambled my thought patterns. "I'm sorry. I'm not thinking clearly."

After a moment, he said, "All ready."

When I turned around, Sven wore a neatly pressed white dress shirt that had the top buttons—the one at the neck and the first one at the chest—undone. His slacks were stiff as a board with razor-sharp creases. He looked svelte. Svelte Sven the Swede. As asinine a comment as I'd ever thought.

"You don't have anything else to wear besides dress clothes?"

Sven frowned like a confused child. "Yeah, I do. Force of habit, I guess."

I shrugged. "Whatever you want to wear is your business."

We got in the car, and he drove across the street to the Holiday Inn. I waited in the Mercedes while he checked in at the desk. Done and back, Sven pulled the car to the far left end of the building. He handed me a keycard in an envelope. Room Number 1112 was written on the sheath in black marker. I could still smell the ink.

He said, "Want to go open the room up while I get my bags?"

"Sure thing."

The parking lot was full, but we were in luck. Sven noticed the reverse lights of a silver BMW. He stopped behind the coupe, backed up, and waited until the car was on its way. Sven pulled in between two church vans. The one on my side was close, and I dinged the paneling with the car door when I opened it, causing me to look around to see if anyone had noticed.

A face in the window of the van almost made me lose control of my bowels. The man was young, with a teardrop tattoo under his left eye. Ex- or current-con, I wasn't sure.

I mouthed, "I'm sorry," and he shrugged, as if to say, "Ain't my van, lady. I just ride in it."

Squeezing out of the ten inches I was allowed, I got out of the car and eased the door shut behind me. I walked through the narrow space between the van and the car until I came to a bleached white section of sidewalk.

There was a door on that side of the building that could be accessed by the keycard I'd been given. I stuck the card into the top, the red light flashed green, and I was allowed inside.

Holding the door open, I called back to Sven, "Do you have a key? You can't get into the building without one!"

He patted the breast pocket of his shirt. "Sure do."

I let the door swing closed behind me and heard the lock snap when it caught. I read the room numbers as I walked down the hall. Room 1112 was about a quarter of the way down on the left of the crimson-carpeted hallway. I used the card to gain entrance.

A cold blast of air welcomed me when I stepped into the room. I could hear the hum of the air conditioning working under the window at the back of the room. Luckily, Sven had gotten a room with two queen-sized beds. I might have made him sleep on the floor otherwise. I stepped into a big bathroom. Triangular-folded towels and washcloths lay in the middle of the counter beside the sink. The arrangement looked like a Trivial Pursuit piece devoid of color. Very artistic, I thought.

I washed my hands in the basin, using the complimentary conch-shaped soap. It smelled of lavender. I immediately regretted the action. I hated the smell of lavender.

Remembering Sven would be close behind me, I went out and put the safety latch in the jamb to prop the door open. I turned back to the beds and realized I didn't have any clothes with me. The thought leaped into my mind like a cannon blast. I even flinched, it'd hit me so hard.

When Sven, lugging a suitcase and a duffel bag, finally walked through the door, I told him my predicament.

"Can it wait until tomorrow? I can buy you some clothes at Walmart or somewhere."

My head was starting to hurt again. I sighed. "I suppose so. I guess I'm sleeping in what I have on, huh? I'm not letting you catch me in my bra and panties, *that's* for sure."

"You saw me in my underwear."

"I, for one, have some class left, Sven. Believe me." I sat down on the edge of the closest bed and rubbed my temples. My lavender-scented hands being in close proximity to my nose only served to make the headache worse. I placed my hands on my knees and leaned back, stretching my tired spine.

Sven scrunched up his face. "Are you trying to say I don't have any class?"

I cast a look of contempt at him. "Not that I've witnessed."

"You know, I'm starting to get used to your abrasive attitude, so I'll let you have a pair of sweat pants and a T-shirt if you want to sleep in those."

I said, "That'll work."

Sven tossed his duffel onto the bed nearest the air conditioning unit and placed his suitcase at the foot of mattress. He unzipped his bag, rummaged inside, and came out with my apparel for the night. He tossed the clothes onto the other bed. "You take the first shower."

I forced a laugh. "I think you need one more than me."

"I'll be fine. I've waited this long."

"You sure?"

"I'm sure."

I could see our time on the road slathered all over his face. He was dirty, tired, and hated being in my company just as much as I despised being in his. Still, he was offering me a kindness that I didn't quite know how to accept. If he was trying to win my good graces, he'd have to try harder than that. "Don't think I don't see what you're doing."

He let out a breath of exasperation. "What now, Ella? Seriously, I don't have it in me to argue with you any more tonight."

I gave him a curt, "Nothing," and went off to the bathroom.

I had my head in the clouds, fussing with thoughts of my prior enemy, Sven. I stepped into the bathroom, not paying much attention to my surroundings. I took off my dirty clothes, bundled them into a ball under my arm, and turned to the mirror.

"Baaaaaaaaaaaaaah!" For the second time in twenty-four hours, I bleated like a God-blessed sheep.

Sven yelled, "You all right in there?"

I was shaken, but I managed, "Yeah. Yeah… well, I don't know."

Written across the mirror in soap was: ASP901465

In the reflection, the shower curtain extended outward. It hovered just over my left shoulder—a ghost in a beige, nylon sheet.

Dane said, "Inside, they reduced me to a number. Never did like numbers. You can have them... if you want."

Doing a piss-poor job of trying to steel myself, I began shaking as if I had a back massager stuck up my hind end. "Go away, Dane."

"Why would I want to do that?"

"This is... this is pointless. You're not gonna hurt me." I prayed that I was right. He hadn't harmed me thus far, so I figured my logic was sound.

"Don't make me prove you wrong, Momma."

I decided on another course of action. In the most motherly voice I could concoct, I growled, "I said... go *away*, Dane!"

One by one, the shower curtain snapped from its rings—*pop... pop... pop*. I remained stoic, figuring Dane would simply bow out, and I'd be left alone. In the mirror, I could make out the contours of Dane's face beneath the material. Equal amounts of fear and pressure built up in my head, becoming immense, too much to bear, as I stood cemented to the floor. I whimpered.

Dane stepped out of the bathtub, still cloaked in his nylon sheet. He growled low in his throat. He sounded like his father. Dane shoved me into the counter, and I grunted as the world exploded into a kaleidoscope of colors.

Sven yelled, "What's going on in there?" He began hammering on the door.

Dane grabbed the back of my head and shoved my face into the countertop. Colors were exchanged for brilliant white light filling my vision. Those black orbs that had haunted me at Talia's drifted in and out of the shimmering ambience.

Dane pulled my head back and slammed my face down again. In a far-off place, I could still hear Sven hollering and the doorknob shaking. But Dane wasn't going to let him in. My son had a point to prove.

He whispered in my ear, "I only need one of you. Now, be a good girl and behave."

The pressure on the back of my skull lifted, and I crumpled as the bathroom door pushed open into me. I ended up in the space between the commode and the bathtub. My entire face throbbed like a thumb caught in a doorjamb.

"My God, Ella! You all right? Oh… your face." Sven sounded so scared I almost laughed.

A line of warm blood ran down the bridge of my nose. Some of it detoured and landed in my right eye. I wiped it away with the back of my hand, then held out my shaking fist and studied the thick crimson on my knuckles. In my mind, I heard Dane's voice again, soft, yet threatening: *Remember, I only need one of you.*

I thought about Talia's ravaged face and counted myself lucky. Dane could have gone much further than he had. I sat there, trembling and sobbing, while Sven shot question after question at me.

Finally acknowledging him, I said, "I tested him. And I lost."

Sven and I decided not to leave each other alone anymore. We retreated into the main room so Sven could gather the clothes he would change into after he washed up. While I showered, Sven held the curtain in place. He might have been a gentleman and not peeked, but I couldn't be sure. The stream of the jet was painful and soothing on my face, all at the same time.

When I was done, Sven backed away from the bathtub but kept the shower curtain up while I toweled off and dressed in the clothes he'd given me. Afterward, I returned the favor, holding the curtain in place while Sven washed away two weeks of muck and mire.

By the time he'd dressed, my arms were sore and shaking from having them up for so long. I dropped the nylon sheet to the floor and massaged my trembling biceps. After Sven shaved, I followed him into the living area of the hotel room.

In the mirror above the dresser, my reflection showed purple bruises had begun to form under my eyes. The gash at my hair line was beginning to coagulate and seal. I looked bad and felt even worse. Whatever safety net I had imagined had been yanked out from under me. Still, a question loomed in the back of my mind: If Dane only needed one of us, why spare both of us for so long?

I wouldn't get my answer that night, so I crawled into bed and nestled into my covers. Sven turned on the TV, and a news report came on about a roadside bombing in Iraq. Three American soldiers had been killed, along with a photojournalist named Mark Simmons who'd been working with the USO. The dead soldiers' names were being withheld out of respect for their families.

Sven said, "Damn. I think I knew that guy. He did an awesome piece back in the early nineties about some crazy cop in Bay's End, Ohio. That's sad. He was a big guy."

Half asleep, I grumbled, "Pretty famous, huh?"

"Not really. I mean big as in huge. The guy was three of me."

"That's big."

"Yep."

I dreamt Talia Stemsford stood in the narrow hallway of her trailer, her smashed countenance grinning at me. From between her legs crawled the woman in the Ravens jersey, her brown hands leaving muddy prints in her wake. I turned to run, to flee the madness, but Stanley the Painter was behind me.

The bullet wound in his neck had grown blue lips. They said, "The teeth'll lead me home."

TWENTY

AS THE YEARS TICKED BY and Dane grew into a man, there were no warning signs as to the person he would become. He never tortured animals that I was aware of, nor did he act out violently in any other fashion.

Well, there was Billy Milson. But that was different.

On Sundays, my family would pile into our Ford LTD station wagon—that wagon would be sold after Phil's death so I could buy my Camry—and we would head off to church. Phil and I would sit in Bible study while Dane went off to Sunday school. It was the rare occasion I didn't have my son at my hip, and I enjoyed my time away from him. He wasn't a bad kid, but every mother deserved a break now and then.

Dane had just hit puberty and was starting to grow facial hair. Thirteen was a difficult age for him. The older Dane got, the harder Phil worked to enforce the importance of being a "man." From what I was told, Dane had been sitting next to twelve-year-old Billy Milson when Billy called Nikki Waldrip—an early blooming, pretty, young girl—a "stupid bitch." Nikki had refused Billy a kiss while the teacher, with her back to the class, scribbled Bible verse explanations on the blackboard. Dane told Billy to shut up, that he shouldn't talk to a girl like that, and Billy called my son a "furry faggot."

For some reason, Dane was sensitive about his peach fuzz. To compound the fact, Billy had challenged Dane's masculinity. Before the teacher could respond to the thrashing young boys in the middle of the class, Dane broke Billy's collarbone and snapped his right wrist so badly that Billy's hand dangled limply from his forearm. The police were called, and Dane was questioned, slapped on the wrist, and left in my care. For all the motherly feelings, I was surprised at the sense of pride I felt. I told Dane he'd done the right thing in protecting a woman, but that he'd gone too far.

Dane looked up at me with cold, brown eyes. "When's enough, Momma? And why doesn't Daddy know when's enough?"

"Your father doesn't know everything, Dane. Neither do I. But you have to be better than your parents." I jumbled myself into that statement because I didn't want Dane to think I was talking solely about his father. "You need to be better and know when to stop."

"I don't get it." Dane's voice had begun to deepen, and he sounded so much like his father then, confusion and all.

"You will."

Lord, was I wrong.

TWENTY-ONE

I AWOKE TO THE SOUND OF the hotel room door closing. Sven nodded at me when I rolled over. He had a plain brown bag tucked under his arm.

He delved inside and came out with a pack of Virginia Slim menthols and a Bic lighter. He tossed them onto the comforter. "Figured you'd need those eventually."

I rubbed my eyes and stretched as I sat up. "I haven't thought about a cigarette since Talia. Funny how watching someone being murdered affects your bad habits."

"Yeah, well…" Sven didn't finish his thought.

I yanked myself out of bed. My entire body was stiff, and my head throbbed. Quasimodo hadn't returned, but I could feel him lurking. I needed some Tylenol.

As luck would have it, the next thing Sven pulled from his magic paper bag was a travel-sized bottle of aspirin. He tore off the safety cellophane and popped the top. He threw the wad of cotton that came with the pills into the trash can by the dresser. He dumped a few pills into his hand, popped them into his mouth, and began chewing.

I grimaced. "Yuck."

"I'm used to it. I get headaches."

"You too, huh? Can I have two?"

Sven walked over to where I sat on the edge of the bed and poured a couple out for me.

"Thanks," I said. I went to the coffee station, grabbed an individually wrapped plastic cup, and allowed myself to go into the bathroom unattended.

Sven showed up in the doorway while I filled the cup in the sink. I realized I'd left him alone in the main room while I'd come to take my medicine. Then again, he'd left me to go shopping.

I took my pills, finishing the water in one big gulp. "What happened to not leaving each other alone?"

"I didn't want to wake you up. Dane didn't bother me."

I nodded, not knowing what else to say. Funny how I didn't think about smoking since leaving Well Being, but when Sven dropped that pack and lighter on the bed, a cigarette was all I could think about. Still, we'd promised to stay together, so I waited, leaning against the door to the hotel room, while Sven packed.

Sven zipped up his suitcase and asked, "Are you just going to stand there and stare at me?"

"I look that anxious, huh?"

"Yeah."

"Well, you wanna stop what you're doing and come outside with me?"

"Go on. I imagine Dane's done for now."

"Kinda going against everything we talked about, aren't we? I'll wait."

"I'm almost done. Just go ahead. I'll meet you at the car." Sven slung his duffel over his shoulder and picked up the suitcase. "I'll go check out, and we'll leave. You won't be alone ten minutes."

"You'll hurry?"

"I'll rush like the wind."

"Fine. Can you make it five minutes instead of ten?"

"Deal."

Sven and I walked out together, but he went left, and I turned right. As I approached the hotel's side door, I could see the Mercedes in its parking place and a man pacing back and forth in front of the door. I pushed open the door and stepped outside.

The man with the teardrop tattoo glanced at me, did a double take, and finally settled his brown eyes on mine. He wore a Dickies khaki button-down with a pair of baggy jeans. If he turned around and lifted his shirt, I was sure I'd have seen a good three inches of his underwear, if not more.

"You all right, lady?" He took a drag off what looked like a rolled cigarette.

The pungent scent of marijuana hit me, and I realized I had been mistaken. "I'm fine, thank you."

He leaned back against the front of the van, a second toke making him barrel-chested until he blew out a light-gray cloud. "You don't look all right. Who whupped up on you?"

I'd forgotten about my black eyes and split hairline. I probably looked the part of a battered girlfriend. I waved him off. "I slipped getting out of the shower."

"Yeah?" His eyes darkened. He pinched the cherry off his joint and rubbed the char onto his pants. The weed went in the pocket of his shirt. "My mother used to fall down the stairs a lot. Only she didn't. You know what I mean?"

I opened my pack of cigarettes while I thought about my next words very carefully. I stuck a Slim between my lips, lit it, and inhaled deeply, trying to act as casual as possible.

I must not have responded quickly enough for the man's liking because he pushed even further. "Your boyfriend come at you?"

"I'm sure it's none of your business." I realized my mistake before I even finished my statement.

He came off the front of the van and took a step toward me. "I didn't see you with anyone else last night. Where is he?"

Sven came out, looking as confused as I was concerned. I didn't have time to warn him. The man with the teardrop tattoo took three quick strides toward Sven, grabbed him by the front of the shirt, and shoved his back to the wall.

Sven yelled, "Hey," as the man slugged him in the gut. Sven's lips clamped together and farted out a great burst of wind.

"You like to hit women, dude? Huh? You gonna answer me, *puta*?" He punched Sven, only higher the second time, in the ribs. "Well, *cabrone*?"

I was stuck. In my head, the man with the tattoo vanished and was replaced by Phil. Sven had become Dane. We were in the kitchen back at my home. Dane had Phil pinned against the fridge, screaming about how he shouldn't have touched his momma.

Teardrop Tattoo reared back, seemingly intent on escalating his targeting to Sven's face. I saw his arm move, saw the muscles in his forearm twitch, meaning to react, but I also witnessed the imprint on his hairy arm, the shape of fingers unmistakable in his flesh.

Dane came on like a film started up at the cinema, much as he had done in Talia's bathroom. He just kind of flickered into existence. Teardrop craned his neck to

164

see who was holding him and had just settled his eyes on Dane when Dane helped the man's head the rest of the way around. Teardrop stood there for a moment, looking like a still frame from *The Exorcist*, with his head facing the wrong direction. And then, he collapsed.

I screamed. Sven was already moving. He reached me, took my arm, and dragged me toward the Mercedes. He left a big scratch on the side of the white van when he pulled the car door open. It was much worse than the little nick I'd left. He all but stuffed me into the passenger seat. I focused on that scratch, not wanting to look at the dead man on the sidewalk.

Sven got in, foul words describing fornication coming out of him in torrents. I did catch a few coherent thoughts mixed in with all the crass language.

"He was taking his teeth at the end. Ella, he was taking his… teeth! They had cameras… cameras all over the place. Oh, God! They had cameras."

I didn't know if that was a good thing or a bad thing. By the frazzled tone of his voice, Sven didn't seem to like the idea. I only wanted to be far away from the corpse with the teardrop tattoo and his head on the wrong way.

Our tires peeled and barked as Sven fled the Holiday Inn's parking lot. We left Goodland, Kansas, in a wake of rubber and fear.

TWENTY-TWO

AT SOME POINT, DANE'S ABUSE became commonplace, but I failed to see when that shift occurred. My reactions to Phil's beating of our son lessened more and more with every instance, until I was reduced to nothing more than a house nurse tending after the child. The more distant I became from my family, the closer I got to God. Besides, I had nowhere to go and no money even if I did find a place.

In the summer of 1990, my mother passed away. I hadn't seen her in three years, not since Dane was four. She had come to visit one afternoon and had seen the bruises on the backs of Dane's legs, the ones Phil left with the broomstick. My mother wasn't one to intrude, but I could see in her eyes that she wanted to say something. She called the next day, pretending she just wanted to talk. The conversation was awkward, and for the most part, I remained silent.

Just before she hung up, she said, "If you ever need anything, call me."

I never took her up on the offer. After that, every time she mentioned dropping by, I made an excuse, saying that we had other plans. After six months of that, she finally stopped offering to visit and just settled for the occasional phone call.

In her will, she left me ten thousand dollars, more than enough for me to take Dane and leave Phil. Actually, she might have intended for me to use the money in just such a way.

In mid-August, two weeks after my mother's death, Phil came to me while I was sulking in our bed, pretending to read a Sue Grafton mystery.

He said, "You need to get out of this house." He went to the closet and started pulling out dresses I hadn't worn in years, fancy numbers that showed off too much, both top and bottom.

"I'm reading." In truth, I was thinking about the easiest way to get away from him for good.

Phil tossed a minidress across my back. "Get dressed. We're going out. I got a surprise for you."

I made my frustration known by sighing heavily. He didn't seem to notice. Not feeling up to arguing with him, I got up and did as I was told.

Dressed and ready, I joined Phil and Dane in the living room. Dane looked dapper in a pale-blue button-down shirt, khakis, and shiny dress shoes. I'd bought the ensemble for him so he could attend my mother's funeral, and realizing that caused my heart to drop a little. Phil had slicked the boy's hair into a swooping comb over. The name "Poindexter" came to mind.

Phil wore the same black shirt and charcoal slacks he'd dressed in for my mother's wake. I knew my husband meant well, but he'd simply not thought their apparel through well enough. Perfunctorily, I complimented them both.

Phil took us to Seaside Bay, an expensive restaurant in the heart of Well Being. For some odd reason, Dane's distaste for seafood didn't cross my mind, or I would have had Phil choose another location.

A timid waitress took Phil's and my orders before switching her attention to Dane. My boy sat there, hands in his lap, shaking his head slowly.

"Speak up," Phil told him. "The lady's waitin'."

Dane blurted, "A salad."

The waitress started, "What kind of dress—"

"You're havin' more than a salad, boy."

Dane mumbled, "I don't want anything else."

"Fine," Phil growled. "Give him the popcorn shrimp kid's plate. And bring me a Coors, will ya?"

It wasn't until the waitress returned with Phil's beer and was gone again that I realized why Dane seemed so meek and quiet.

I leaned over and whispered to him, "Just try to eat some of it, okay?"

He nodded but never took his eyes off his father.

Our meals came a little less than thirty minutes later. I enjoyed my lobster while Phil devoured his baked salmon. From the corner of my eye, I watched Dane secret away a piece of fried shrimp under his right hip. I wanted to say something, but I had no course of action with Phil sitting directly beside me. All I could do was sit and eat. Hopefully, Phil would get up to use the restroom at some point.

Five beers and a full meal later, Phil hadn't budged an inch. The check came, and he paid with a wad of twenties from his wallet. Shocked at the magnitude of cash he was carrying, I forgot all about Dane.

I asked Phil, "Where'd you get all that?"

"The bank. Where else I'ma get money from?"

"The only thing we have left this month is…" And just like that, it hit me. "You withdrew my mother's money, didn't you?"

He smiled. "Surprise! Paid off the last eight grand on the house, too. They gave me an option that knocked over five thousand off the final... What the hell you lookin' at me like that for?"

"That was *my* money, Phil."

His smile died a fiery death on his face. "Oh, so this here's *your* money. Was it *your* money that's been payin' the bills up to this point? Huh? Go on, answer me."

I shook my head. "I don't believe you."

"I did this for you, Ella. You need'ta show me some gratitude. Lookit this way. No more mortgage payment."

Flabbergasted, I sat back in stunned silence. I'd suffered the man for years, dealt with a monster I couldn't afford to be without, and he'd managed to ruin my escape plan without even realizing it.

Standing up, Phil said, "You ready?"

I didn't say a word. I tried to move, but my body wouldn't listen to my brain's commands. Phil waited all of two seconds before heading for the main aisle of the restaurant. To reach the front of the establishment, he had to walk behind Dane. He slowed, his eyes homing in on the floor next to his son's chair. Following his gaze, I saw two shrimp that had escaped from under Dane's hip to land on the polished hardwood.

Phil put his hand on Dane's shoulder and squeezed until his knuckles blanched. "Get. Up."

"Phil..." I trailed off as I scanned the dining area. If Phil managed to make a scene, maybe the cops would come.

But my husband was too smart for that.

With his father's hand still vise-like on his collarbone, Dane rose from his seat. Three more shrimp fell, bouncing and dancing across the shiny floor. At least ten more pieces remained on the cushion, having been smashed into the upholstery by Dane's bottom.

"Oh," Phil said, "you done did it now, boy." He led Dane out of the restaurant by the back of his son's neck with me following close behind.

On the drive home, Phil stayed oddly quiet. He picked at his teeth every now and then, even turned the stereo on to a talk radio program, but never said a word. When we got home, Phil retired to the bedroom while I waited for Dane to get into his pajamas. Once he was ready, I tucked him in, said the Lord's Prayer with him, and kissed him goodnight.

Phil was asleep by the time I slid into bed. I'd been expecting a beating of epic proportions to befall my son, but it never came. I drifted off, relieved that the subject was closed.

The next morning, I got up and started my Saturday ritual of cooking breakfast for my family. I set the table with steaming plates and called to Phil and Dane, telling them everything was ready. Phil came in, lively and more awake than I'd ever seen him on a weekend morning, and sat down to eat. Dane arrived a few minutes later, still rubbing sleep out of his eyes. A line of toothpaste-laden drool stained the side of his chin.

Without saying a word, Phil swiped Dane's plate onto the kitchen floor. Dane jumped back as hot grits and eggs splattered his pajama legs.

I blurted, "What did you do that for?"

Phil pointed his fork at me. "You, shuddup." His gaze drifted over to Dane. "Now, you, clean that mess up and go get ready for your day."

I said, "He needs to eat."

"He shoulda thought about that before wasting his food last night." Phil went back to his own food, stuffing his cheeks full, but not taking his eyes off Dane.

"Momma?" Dane whined.

"What you talking to her for? Didn't I just give you an order?"

Dane ignored his father, keeping his eyes on me. Phil started to get up.

"Do what your father says, Dane."

I was trying to save him another beating, but Dane just stared at me, a deflated look about him. His bottom lip trembled. Something inside me tightened, making it hard to breathe.

Phil exploded, "Now, boy!"

Dane left in hurry, nothing but a blur of pajamas and hair.

For lunch, I made Dane a peanut butter and jelly sandwich. Phil sat at the kitchen table, reading a copy of *Trains* magazine. Dane was outside, playing in the backyard, so I rolled open the sliding glass door and hollered for him. He ran across the grass, beaming at the word "lunch." He slid past me into the kitchen. When I turned around, Phil was up and standing beside the counter, ogling Dane's sandwich.

"I think this is yours," Phil said, picking up the PB&J.

I stood dead still as Dane approached his father. Phil stalked backward until he came to the trash can. My son reached for the sandwich. Phil crushed Dane's lunch into a dripping ball and tossed it into the bin.

Phil grinned. "There's always supper, huh?"

That night, Phil told me to make pot roast for dinner—Dane's favorite. I slaved in the kitchen for two hours preparing and cooking that meal. Knowing Dane hadn't eaten all day, I poured my heart and soul into the recipe. We all sat down at the table in front of our meals, and Phil said grace for the first time ever.

"Dear God, let this food nourish our tummies and make us strong. And while we eat, let my son see the error of his ways. In Jesus's name, amen."

Relief washed over me in cool waves. Phil was finally going to let Dane get some food in his stomach.

Dane reached for his fork. Phil's arm shot out, his hand brandishing his own fork, and stabbed the boy in the forearm. Dane squealed. The boy's fork slid off the table and landed on the floor, tinkling as it skittered across the linoleum.

Phil grinned. "Who said you could eat?"

"But you—"

"I didn't say nothin' about you in that there prayer. I was talkin' 'bout your mother and me. We need all the strength we can muster, what with having to deal with an unappreciative li'l twerp like you."

"Phil, let him—"

Phil stuck his fork in my face for the second time that day. "What'd I tell you 'bout underminin' me?"

Like a good wife, I clammed up.

Bedtime came, and Dane didn't get a single morsel of food. The rest of the night, Phil hadn't allowed me anywhere near the kitchen. More than once, he told me, "Don't even think about it," as if he could read my mind and knew I wanted to sneak some food to my son.

I finally gave up and went to bed. When I got up the next morning, my husband was in the same place I'd left him—sitting on the couch watching TV. From the deep, dark pockets under his eyes, I assumed he'd stayed up all night to keep me from sneaking any food to Dane.

Sunday was no different. I fixed more of Dane's favorite meals for breakfast, lunch, and dinner, only for Phil to deprive our son of a single ounce of sustenance.

Monday morning, Phil was on the couch again, but he'd actually crashed. In the kitchen, I quickly made Dane a ham sandwich. Finishing up, I stuffed the mayo and the lunch meat back into the fridge and closed the door.

Phil stood in the doorway to the living room, yawning. He nodded at the sandwich. "Hope you plan on eatin' that."

Trying to change the subject, I said, "Why aren't you at work?"

"Called in sick. Figure I could use a day or two of vacation now that the house is paid off." He took two steps toward me. I took one step back. We danced like that until my back hit the sliding glass door.

Phil smiled. Tenderly, he pulled the sandwich from my grasp and took a large bite out of the corner. "Ham," he said. "Not my fav, but it'll do."

"You're starving him, Phil. You do realize that, don't you? They'll throw you in jail... for a long time."

"He'll survive," he said with a smirk. "I did."

Phil left me alone in the kitchen to ponder what he meant by that last statement.

Dane didn't eat again until Wednesday.

TWENTY-THREE

SVEN DIDN'T LIKE THE IDEA of staying in Kansas any longer than necessary, what with the corpse we'd left behind at the Holiday Inn. According to the GPS on his phone, the Oklahoma state line was closer than driving into Missouri. He said we could shave off four hours by taking Interstate 70 to I-135 into Oklahoma.

Sven also felt we should get rid of the Mercedes. I didn't argue. While he drove, he gave me directions on how to work the search function built into his cell. I hunted down a buy-here-pay-here place in Blackwell, Oklahoma, about thirty miles over the state line.

When we reached Arkansas City, Kansas, Sven pulled off the interstate and went to a Bank of America I'd found on the GPS. I waited in the car while he went inside to do his business.

He came out holding a gray plastic bag. He got back into the car and dropped the satchel into my lap. "There's five thousand in there. I'm sure we'll be able to snag something for that. I doubt these mom-and-pop used-car places will take a check, much less a credit card."

I nodded. The man was smarter than I had given him credit for. I supposed, though, even brilliant men had bouts with stupidity every now and then.

I'd never been to that section of Oklahoma, but it was much different than I'd assumed. The land was flat and plain. We passed field after field bereft of life. November didn't look like a prosperous month for the state. We'd left death behind only to find ourselves surrounded by it in Oklahoma.

After seven hours on the road—not including the stop at Bank of America—we stopped to eat at a Palace Pies in Blackwell. The restaurant was fifteen minutes off the interstate and completely dead. Beside the vehicles parked around back in what I figured was the employee parking area, ours was the only car there.

We got out, and Sven locked the car with his key fob. The car's horn bleated twice, and I about jumped right out of my skin. Needless to say, I was still on edge.

A young, dark-skinned girl welcomed us when we walked into the restaurant. I checked the clock above the cash register—5:13, much later than I thought. I hadn't paid a great deal of attention to the readout on Sven's car stereo, but I'd been sure it was an hour earlier, at least. Then, I remembered the time change. We'd played Marty McFly and gone back to the future.

I nudged Sven's elbow as he perused the menu above the girl's head. "That car place is going to be closed." I pointed at the clock.

Sven nodded. "I'd anticipated that. We're going to have to try it anyway."

The girl said, "Most places 'round here don't get done 'til 'bout six or seven. Folks work late in these parts." She shrugged. Her eyes stayed on me a fraction of a second longer than I was comfortable with. I noticed she had startling blue eyes. I figured they were contacts. Her gaze darted away. Then I remembered the

176

state of my face—the gash at my hairline and the dark bruises under my eyes. I suddenly knew how Dane had felt all those years, hiding the aftereffects of Phil's abuse from the outside world.

"Thanks for the information," I said.

"So what can I get you?" A smile wider than the Rockies were tall stitched itself across her face. Her teeth glowed a brilliant white. They were the kind of teeth Dane would love.

The thought caught me so off guard that my breath hitched, and a tiny strand of saliva caught in the back of my throat. I started coughing. I tried to keep my hand over my mouth, but the convulsions were too strong. I bent over, sucking wind, and placed my hands on my knees.

"Here. Here," the girl said. I managed to look up and saw she'd made me a cup of something. "On the house."

I snatched the cup out of her hand and took three healthy gulps of an overly sweet, syrupy substance. The fluid coated my throat, and my coughing abated. "What is this?"

She looked at me funny, tilting her head like a puppy told to sit. "Tea."

"It's so… sweet."

"That's how we like it 'round here."

Sven asked me, "You all right now?"

"Fine. Did you decide what you wanted while I was dying?"

"Will pepperoni and black olives work?"

I nodded. "Toss some mushrooms and sausage on there, and you have a deal."

"Bleck! I hate mushrooms."

The girl smiled. "I can put caps on her side only."

177

"Caps?" I asked.

Sven told me, "She means mushrooms." To the girl, he said, "Spend a lot of time in the Windy City?"

"Yes!" she squealed. Her excitement made me smile. She seemed so fresh and innocent. I missed being young. "My dad lives there." Her nose wrinkled. "I don't see him much anymore. He got remarried."

She went on to tell us about how her father began ignoring her after his new wife got pregnant. I tried to pay attention, tried even harder to care, but I didn't do either with much gusto. I hadn't eaten in over twenty-four hours, and my stomach was speaking much louder than the girl across the counter ever could.

Sven and I took a booth at the back of the establishment. I hated to sit down again, so I excused myself to go outside and have a smoke.

Sven said, "Be careful."

"There's windows everywhere. You'll be able to watch me."

I walked out, passing the counter girl on the way. She waved and showed me her pearly whites again. I didn't want to think about how much Dane would like them, but I did.

I chain-smoked three Slims. I half-expected my son to make himself known while Sven and I were separated. My heart raced. I didn't know if the cause was my fear of Dane popping up or the nicotine working its way into my bloodstream. I butted the last smoke in the ashtray-slash-trashcan by the door and went back inside. The aromas of baking marinara sauce and cooking meats mixed with the cloud of smoke that still clung to my hair and clothes smelled amazing, something a non-smoker would never understand.

When I got to the table, the counter girl stood at our booth. Our half-and-half pizza steamed in the center of the table. My stomach roared.

She and Sven were discussing Chicago and deep-dish delights. She told him about a vacation in New York she'd taken in her senior year of high school and how she'd hated their thin-crust monstrosities. Sven agreed with her, stating that his hometown's pies were the best in the country. I'd never been to Chicago or New York, so I ignored their conversation and began eating.

While they talked, I ravaged two thick slices of pizza. I was full to the brim even as I devoured the crust of my second piece. I had been sure that I could have consumed my entire half, but my stomach seemed to have shrunk. That was for the best. I didn't need to be riding—or driving—while stuffed to the gills, if Sven saw fit when we switched cars.

A couple with a young boy in tow entered, calling our counter girl away from her conversation with Sven. She waved at the group, saying giddily, "How y'all doin' tonight?"

Sven picked up a piece of pizza and took a bite. Grease rolled down the crease of his chin. He wiped it away with a napkin taken from the box at the wall. He chewed and swallowed, then said, "I like the way she talks."

"She sounds like Dane. The accent, I mean, not that bubbly personality."

"I've been meaning to ask you about that." He cleaned his hands with a moist towelette he'd snatched from a rack beside the napkin dispenser.

"About what?"

"I've been to Colorado on several occasions, and I know you were born there because of my research into your family, but I've never heard anyone around there talk like Dane. I always chalked it up to his time driving trucks, but I'm assuming there's another reason that eludes me."

"Dane's father, Phil—"

"Sorry about your loss, by the way. I know he died… what, ten years ago now?"

"That's about right. Just before Dane went on his… journey. Anyway, my husband was a born Georgian. He spent his rearing days around the most country folks you've ever seen in your life. His family was a backwoods sort. And you know what they say, 'You can take the boy out of the country, but you can't take the redneck out of the man.'"

"Right. I've heard something like that." Sven shoved the last of his first slice into his mouth. He grabbed another piece before he'd even swallowed.

"Well, Dane caught on to the way his father spoke. I hated it, but I guess a part of Dane wanted to be like his old man. He grew into a man far more violent than his father, though. I homeschooled Dane, so he rarely got around decent-speaking people."

"Phil ever beat you?"

"He didn't raise his hand to me as much as he did Dane. The last time I saw Dane outside of a courtroom, my son had defended me against his father. Phil got riled up over a promotion I got, one that had me making more money then him, so he hit me. Dane threw Phil's butt through our sliding glass door."

Sven latched onto his slice, ripped a piece the size of my hand off, and seemed to swallow it whole. After the section started its journey to his stomach, he asked, "How long did Dane suffer Phil's abuse?"

I almost didn't answer. A part of me didn't want to air my dirty laundry, but I also felt it was time to tell someone. "All the while he was growing up. Phil ramped up the beatings when the boy started growing hair in new places."

Sven let out a burst of laughter. "That's one way of skirting the word puberty. So, Dane had… *the change,* and things got worse?"

"That's about right."

"Did you ever do anything to stop it?"

Without thinking, I blurted, "No."

Sven sat there a moment with a look in his eyes I couldn't figure out. I thought maybe he was judging me, putting me low on the evolutionary chain, like some cave-dwelling, pile-of-crap mother.

I added, "I was scared."

"I'm sure it wasn't all cupcakes and rainbows for Dane, either, but I get what you're saying. I wasn't in your shoes, so I have no way of knowing how I would have reacted. Still, I have to wonder what Dane might have been like if you'd just disappeared with him one night."

Anger swelled in my breast, but I tried my best to remain calm. "And take him where, Mr. Gödel?"

"There's that 'Mr. Gödel' nonsense again. Look, *Ella May Peters*, we're in this together, whether you like it or not, so pardon me if I want to know everything about what I've been thrust into. If you were a horrible mother, then fine. No one can change any of that now. I might have crossed the line in insinuating that Dane's killing spree was because of you, but you really have no right to be upset. I'm just as screwed as you are. You don't see me arguing with you over the articles I wrote, do you? No, you do not. I've made my bed, and now I will either lay in it or die in it."

As much as I wanted to argue, Sven was actually right. There was no use in checking the rearview mirror. Hindsight wasn't just twenty-twenty; it was also cemented in place, unmovable, unchanging. Dane didn't seem to be looking for an apology. My son meant to make Sven and me suffer. So we had one of two choices: Kill ourselves and be done with it or find out what Dane wanted. Suicide was a sin in my book, as well as in the good Lord's book, so I would wait and allow God to shepherd me out of this mess, if He saw fit.

Sven ate his third and fourth slices of pizza in silence. I allowed him some quiet time. I had nothing more to say on the subject anyway. He ordered a Sprite for the road, and I took an unsweetened iced tea — no more swampy syrup for me. I had a smoke before getting in the car, unsure whether or not Sven would let me partake of my habit in there.

TWENTY-FOUR

PHIL DIED ON A COLD night in January of 2003. I woke up to a gurgling sound, sure that the noise was nothing more than water in the pipes or a bubbling from the toilet. I swung out of bed and even walked into the bathroom before realizing that the sound was coming from behind me.

I flipped the light. Phil lay on his back, his hands clutching his chest. His lips were blue. No worry was present in my heart. He was dying, and though I knew the proper course of action, I made no attempt to help him. I retrieved a dining room chair from the kitchen and placed it beside the bed. I sat and watched my husband pass away.

Being a nurse, I'd seen many people move on from our plane of existence. Phil was no different. He was just another stranger fleeing in the night. He didn't look at me while he went; his eyes remained transfixed on a spot above him. He squinted several times. I assumed he did that when the pain became too much to handle.

The digital clock on my nightstand read three fifteen. I lit a cigarette and leaned back in my chair. I thought about what we'd become to each other. In the three years since Dane had left home, Phil and I simply coexisted. Early on in Phil's sickness, the only times we actually spent together were at his doctor visits. But once he reached a point where he could no longer take more than five steps without becoming short of breath, I took over his daily needs. I was, after all, his wife. Seeing to him was my duty — for sicker and poorer, and all that good stuff. When I wasn't looking after him, I was reading. My collection of unread books at home dwindled, and I resorted to library raids at least once a week. That was how I first met Talia. Every now and then, I'd even read to Phil. It was more to slay the silence that had taken over our house than for his enjoyment.

At 3:24, Phil's chest rattled. He exhaled and never took another breath. I leaned forward and closed his eyes with the palm of my hand.

The smell of urine and feces hit my nose. I'd have to replace our mattress before I slept on it again.

I waited until sunup to call emergency services. Phil had been dead three hours by then. I told the responding paramedics and officers that I'd risen with the sun and found Phil dead when I rolled over. No questions were asked, so my lies remained few. After all, how often did spouses wake up to dead partners? It would seem quite often indeed. The ambulance driver expressed his condolences, as did the EMT who had arrived with him. The officer that came had me sign the report and left without expressing his concern for my loss. I liked that cop. I fancied the notion that somewhere in the back of his mind he'd known exactly what had happened but hadn't said anything.

For the first time since Dane had left home, I tried to find him. I did internet searches at the library for his name, even paid a person-locating service, but nothing came of it. Dane, for all intents and purposes, was off the grid. He had no home address, no credit cards, not even a simple bank account.

I did not weep at my husband's funeral, but I smoked eight cigarettes before they lowered him into the ground. A few of the men Phil used to work with at the rail yard came but had little to say. I received the mandatory, "I'm sorry for your loss," and "Phil was a great guy," before they shuffled off to parts unknown, never to be seen by me again.

Phil's life insurance from his retirement plan paid in full. I sat on one hundred thousand dollars after funeral costs—a security blanket that Phil could never have offered me in life. He left Dane zip, zilch, zero, but I hadn't expected him to, so that wasn't a problem. I sold the Ford LTD station wagon and bought my Camry. I decided on a gold car. It made me feel important.

TWENTY-FIVE

UNBEKNOWNST TO ME, SVEN HAD made plans. While he followed the direction on the phone's GPS, he told me he'd called ahead to the used car lot while I'd been smoking outside Palace Pies. A guy named Rudy had told Sven they were open until eight o'clock that night. So Sven felt there was enough time for a shopping trip.

Off the main road that ran through Blackwell, he turned into a small business with "Dabney's Attic" as a moniker. The sign was tie-dyed, all bright yellows, blues, reds, and greens. The place was no more than a faux-brick building with a glass storefront. The name "attic" was lost on me, as the shop was only one story and seemed to have everything for sale on the main floor.

Once inside, I realized most of the apparel had come secondhand, more than likely from people's attics. I figured the name of that establishment fit after all. Dabney's Attic was run by none other than Dabney herself. The thin, elderly woman—maybe seventy by the lines that creased her face—wore a blue house dress, possibly a Sunday's finest once upon a happily ever after. Her gnarled hands, the knuckles bent and twisted at sharp angles by years of suffering through arthritis, were in stark contrast to the rest of her soft, pliable body. She did, however, use those hands to shake Sven's along with mine.

"Thank you for coming. I do love new customers." Her voice was light, like a blue jay singing spring tunes for the world to appreciate over a glass of lemonade. "Feel free to look around. I'll be just there." She pointed at a barstool that sat next to a bookshelf with an old-fashioned cash register perched atop it. "Come see me when you've found what you're looking for or if you have any questions." She smiled, all big and bold, with teeth the shade of infected urine. I smelled stale smoke and assumed she partook in the same habit I cherished.

Rows of chest-high racks ran the length of the shop. Ratty old clothes, mixed in with newer, brighter items, hung from various types of hangers. The left side of the store was for men, the right for women, and in the back, children's clothes.

Dabney hummed "Amazing Grace" while Sven and I perused her wares. I recalled singing my own terrified, toneless version of that song weeks prior, while Stanley spray-painted the side of my house. I felt unsettled. The more uncomfortable I felt, the louder Dabney's voice seemed to become. I couldn't concentrate.

Sven asked, "Are you okay?"

I whispered, "It's her humming."

"What humming?"

His response stalled my pulse. My heart went into my throat, and I couldn't breathe. I was sure I'd died some time ago, and my body had just found out. Ice coursed through my veins, though, proving I was still alive.

Dabney said, "This is a lot harder than it seems, Momma. No worries, though. I'll leave the old woman be. Find you something proper to wear."

Finally able to breathe again, I grabbed Sven's shirt sleeve. "Sven, I want to go."

"What? *Why*? You need clothes."

"That old woman isn't right."

Sven glanced over his shoulder at Dabney, who was no longer humming or speaking in my son's voice. "She's fine. What's wrong with you?"

"What if… what if Dane's learned how to… take people over?"

Sven shuddered. "Why would you say something like that?"

"You didn't hear her? You really didn't?"

"I wouldn't play games with you, Ella. I didn't hear anything."

From Dabney's mouth, or maybe just in my own confused head, I heard Dane say, "Maybe you've finally lost it, Momma."

I said, "Yeah, maybe."

Sven sighed. "Maybe what?"

"Something's wrong here. Don't look at me like I've gone crazy."

"Somebody has to remain grounded. I didn't hear anything, so calm down. Here, pick out your clothes, and let's get out of here."

Rushing through the store, I chose a turtleneck sweater, two silk blouses, three T-shirts, and four pairs of jeans. I didn't try on a single item, though Sven suggested I should. I ignored his protests and took my garments to the front.

Dabney smiled. "Find everything okay?"

"Sure thing."

Her bent fingers punched the steel buttons of the old-timey register. My total was forty-two dollars. Sven paid cash. Dabney loaded a K-Mart bag with my purchases. I snatched the bag from her and headed for the door.

Sven called after me, "Whoa, Speed Racer! Slow down."

Dabney's voice came next. "Have a good day... Momma."

I spun around and saw Sven coming toward me.

Over his shoulder, Dabney smiled her tea-colored smile. She placed her hands upon her cheeks and made her mouth into an O. Though her lips never moved, I heard Dane's voice clearly as it came out of her. "The teeth'll lead me home."

Sven reached for me, but I was already backing out of Dabney's House of Horrors. I couldn't take my eyes off the old woman while she did her best impression of Macaulay Culkin as Kevin McCallister in *Home Alone*.

I about ripped the passenger side door off in my haste to get into the car.

Sven got in a second behind me, his face a map of confusion and worry. "What did you see?"

"Nothing. Just drive. Please, just get us away from here."

Acquiescing to my pleas, Sven pulled out of Dabney's and, according to the GPS, headed north.

We pulled into Lakeside Auto at a quarter 'til seven. The sun had dropped behind the low, flat lands, leaving a dull, orange-into-purple fan in its wake.

A tall beast of a man in a yellow sweater and blue jeans introduced himself as Rudy as soon as we got out of the car. He smelled strongly of Old Spice and, oddly enough, garlic. Maybe it was just the pizza working its way out of my own pores, but I could have sworn Rudy was trying to ward off Dracula or something of that nature.

Dusty, ill-kept cars were parked in a V formation inside the lot. Every type of vehicle, from minivans to sports cars, sat waiting for a buyer, like pound animals looking for an owner. Strangely enough, I felt bad for those lifeless piles of fiberglass and metal. They seemed lonely.

Rudy's eyes flitted over my face, seemingly assessing my bruised mug, but like the girl back at the pizza place, he didn't mention my condition.

I expected Rudy to sound like Dane when he spoke, but aside from the country accent, Rudy's voice was unfamiliar. "What can I do you for?"

Sven said, "I'm the guy that called earlier. I need something under four grand. You told me you could help."

Rudy grinned, reaching up to play with a gold loop chain around his neck that I hadn't noticed before his fingers found it. "I got everything. That is, everything on the lot's less than four grand, or right at it if'n you're paying cash."

"Cash I have."

"Then we can do bid'ness, partner. Y'all from around here?"

"Nope. We're passing through. I need to get my lady a car, and the girl at the Palace Pies said you had them cheap. My wife's starting college up in Chicago. We're from Texas. Thought I would find something cheaper on the road than the cutthroats I found at home." Sven was a good liar. Absently, I wondered how many untruths he'd slipped past me while we'd been riding together.

"Little old for studyin', ain't'cha, miss?"

I frowned a bit at his rudeness. "Never too late to learn something new." Then I added, "I want to be a

191

nurse. We—my husband and I—just came into some money. Figured now was the time. He's going overseas, so I'll be home alone while he's away. Learning is an easy way to pass time until he gets back." Seemed I was just as good as Sven in the area of fables.

"From Texas, you say?"

Sven answered, "Yes. Lubbock area. Ever been there?"

Rudy ignored the question. "You don't sound like you're from Texas."

Sven quirked an eyebrow. "Is that going to stop you from selling me a car?"

I jumped in before Sven became too aggravated. "We're Army. We move a lot. That's why he's going overseas."

"Ah, that would splain it. S'pose you wanna start looking, huh?"

Sven smiled at me and told Rudy, "That would be nice, yes."

We ended up picking a blue Nissan Maxima with a sun roof. The price, emblazoned on the windshield in numbers with fire coming out of the top of them, was $3,449. Sven talked Rudy down to thirty-two hundred cash. Sven grabbed the money out from under the car seat where I'd stuffed it and went inside to sign the paperwork. I remained in the lot, smoking.

Two women arrived when I was halfway through my second cigarette. They parked their old, busted-up Chevy pickup on the road instead of in the lot. One was heavyset with slumped shoulders, dressed like a man in a wife-beater and blue jeans. She had a man's gait, as well. Her hair was styled into a crew cut with two-inch spikes sticking up from her bangs. The other woman was just as large, but her clothes were more feminine.

Her silk blouse even showed a little cleavage. They both looked to be in their forties and seemed to be a couple.

The manly one approached me and asked, "You work here now? Where's Rudy?"

"Just shopping," I said politely. "Rudy is in with my husband."

She hitched her chin at me, grabbed the other woman's hand, and shuffled off toward the trailer. Before the two women made it there, Sven appeared in the doorway, thanking Rudy over his shoulder. Sven went directly to the Nissan he'd just purchased. He had a screwdriver in one hand and a sheet of what looked like glossy paper and a plastic frame in the other.

I asked him, "What's that?"

"They give temporary plates down here so the police don't give you grief." Sven set to work placing the paper in the frame and attaching it to the rear of the car. When he was done, he laid the screwdriver on the trunk of the brown Ford Escort next to our new car. "He told me to leave it there." He dug into his right front pocket and came out with a set of keys. He tossed them to me. "She's all yours."

"I don't have my license on me, remember?"

"We're going to have to drive out of here with both cars. We'll leave the Mercedes somewhere secluded. Until then, you have to drive. No other choice."

"And what if Dane wants to roll me into a ditch?"

"Do we have any other options?"

"For the record, I don't like this."

"Doesn't really matter what either of us likes. Let's go."

The Nissan wasn't much different from my Camry. I'd driven plenty of cars that were unknown to me in my day and had always seemed to find the brakes too touchy or the steering too light for my liking. Not that Nissan. I settled right in with no trouble.

I followed the Mercedes onto the road, leaving Rudy and the two women behind.

Thirty miles north of Lakeside Auto—which didn't reside by any lake that I was aware of—Sven pulled off into a cornfield. I stayed beside the car and took the opportunity to light up. Ten minutes went by before Sven showed up in the space between the cornstalks the Mercedes had left. His suitcase was in one hand and the duffel over his shoulder. I popped the trunk, and he put everything inside. Instead of getting out and walking around the car, I climbed over the center console and sat in the passenger seat. Sven got in a moment later with his miniature cannon clutched by the barrel in his right hand.

I said, "That thing again? Where's it been all this time?"

"I put it in the trunk when I stopped to drain my... stopped to urinate behind that Dairy Queen in Goodland. I didn't want to leave it behind. Here, put it in the glovebox."

I opened the box and gingerly took the gun between my finger and my thumb. "I never have liked those things," I said, putting the gun carefully in the compartment and closing the door.

"Yeah, well, that *thing* saved you from a nasty bump on your head."

"I still can't figure why Stanley wanted me dead."

Sven put the Nissan into gear and left the roadside in a trail of red dust, made that color by the taillights. "Was that the name of the guy I shot?"

I forgot I hadn't filled Sven in on who Stanley was. I told him the story about the graffiti and how Stanley's company had been the one I'd called to paint over it.

"You mean he was one of the guys painting your house the day I dropped off the DVD?"

"Yep. Things kind of went… downhill after that."

Sven laughed, a truly mirthful sound. "You can say that again."

After forty minutes of driving back roads, he followed the GPS's instructions back to the interstate. The day wore on me, and at some point, I fell into a deep, fitful sleep.

When I woke up, we were parked in the breakdown lane. Red and blue lights spun around me. I looked at Sven. He'd taken the gun from the glovebox. It rested on his lap.

I sat up in my seat. "Where are we? What's happening?"

"I was speeding. I got pulled over. Go figure."

I pointed at the cannon on his lap. "And what do you think you're going to do with that?" I had an image of Stanley's throat whistling with every failed breath he took.

"I don't know yet."

"You're *not* going to kill a cop. Or anyone else for that matter. Where are we?"

"Middle of Missouri. Between Lebanon and St. Robert, on I-44."

"All right. Think about this. How much of a chance do you think there is that they're looking for us? In a whole other state, at that."

When he looked at me, his face was purple from the lights. "Pretty good chance."

"It takes a while for cops to check cameras and such, right? I mean, they need a search warrant, right? *Right*?"

"In the case of the guy with the teardrop, you mean? No. They have probable cause to search the cameras on site immediately."

"What if they were dummy cameras?"

"Highly unlikely, Ella." Sven checked the rearview mirror.

A shadow passed through the spinning azure lights. I looked through the back driver's side window. A cop hugged the side of the Nissan, approaching slowly.

My heart was about to explode. I could see Sven's pulse thudding in the carotid in his neck. I snatched the gun off Sven's lap, threw it to the floor, and kicked it under my seat while the cop was in the blind spot.

The officer rapped on the rear driver's side window with his knuckles. Sven rolled down his window.

The officer said, "Unlock the back door." His voice was awfully familiar.

I whispered, "What's he doing?"

"I'm not asking any questions. We're in enough trouble as it is. You better hope we don't need that gun." Sven growled low in his throat to punctuate his frustration at me. He used the door controls to unlock the back.

The back door popped open, and the dome light came on. The officer flopped onto the backseat and closed the door so quickly I didn't get a look at his face. He slid over until he sat in the middle. "Good. So you can hear me now, Sven."

"I could hear you the entire time, Officer."

"Couldn't hear me back at the old woman's place. Funny how this shit works sometimes and not others."

"What? Sir… I don't understand."

"Quit that 'sir' crap, Sven. Momma, turn around and look at me."

The dome light flickered on of its own accord.

Sven said, "*Momma?*" He twisted around in his seat so that he could look into the rear of the car.

Not wanting to, but knowing I would face the consequences should I decide to buck Dane's orders, I did the same.

Officer Driver stared back at me in the glow of the interior lights. His jaw was slack, and his crystal-blue eyes were empty. A fat line of drool rolled over the corner of Driver's bottom lip and crept slowly down the side of his chin, leaving behind a slimy, glistening trail. If not for the pulse throbbing in Driver's neck, I would have thought the man was one of the living dead. Though just as handsome with his face rugged and carved of stone, the man who'd spoken to me at the library was not in attendance. In spastic movements, Dane made Driver roll his neck, as if loosing the muscles there. "I'm still getting used to this. Nifty trick, huh, Momma?"

"Not him, Dane. Please." All I could think of was Driver's little girl, Helena.

Sven said, "So you can *use* people now, Dane. Is that it?"

"Kinda obvious, isn't it?"

"I guess so."

I said, "You had him follow us all this way?"

"He's been driving all day. A real trooper, this one. I decided to snatch him up, since him and Stanley spray-painted your wall. Remember, Momma, there were two people outside your house. You were sure of it."

I remembered the look Driver had given Officer Sherwood that night, as if I'd deserved the vandalism. I couldn't believe I'd trusted Driver. He'd been so kind to me at the library. I'd made a fool out of myself.

Dane continued speaking through Driver, like a ventriloquist holding a dummy. "I want that dumbass who's driving to slow down. I have things to do and stuff to prepare, but here Sven goes driving all crazy-like, and I gotta come to the rescue… again."

Though Dane spoke clear as day, Driver's mouth never moved. Not once. The sight sent icy snakes slithering through my guts.

I asked, "Is that what you think you did back at the hotel? Rescue me?"

Dane laughed. Driver showed no emotion. "No doubt."

The officer's gaping maw was unsettling, but I continued to stare at it. I figured at any moment, Dane would start moving the guy's mouth, completing the dummy act.

As if reading my mind—and maybe he could, as I had no way of knowing— Dane said, "I can't seem to get used to folks' mouths. Hard to talk with all your teeth in your head. Odd."

"I can slow down, Dane," Sven said, "but this policeman has probably been reported missing, right? They'll be looking for him… for us. There's bound to be a dashboard cam in that car of his."

The officer raised a limp wrist, and Dane made him wave Sven off. "I had him call in at work. Officer Driver here caught jury duty. Now, how to punish you?"

"Punish us?" I asked. "Why do you have to punish us?"

"Because that's how the world goes. Someone does something wrong, and you punish them. Sven's been a bad boy, so now I have to decide how to punish you. You are" — Dane made the officer do air quotes — "*in this together*, right?"

Dane had been watching us, lurking in the shadows for everything we'd said, everything we'd done. Incredulously, I wondered if Dane had been there for Sven's strip tease behind Dairy Queen and my unclean thoughts. Was there nowhere we could turn to be out of my son's presence?

Dane kept Driver's hands up after the air quotes. The eyes shifted in that slack face and latched onto the gold wedding band the officer wore on his ring finger. "What have we here?"

Dane used the officer's hand to reach under him. The body thrust its pelvis up in one quick jerk. I was reminded of a puppet show from my youth where the amateur controlling the marionettes had been horribly unskilled. Dane had the officer remove his wallet. He flopped it open, and a strung-together section of plastic came rolling out. Under the cellophane protection, little Helena smiled, her shimmering brown hair cascading over her shoulders. She had a large gap between her front teeth, but that didn't lessen the beauty of her smile. Behind Helena, a beautiful Samoan-looking woman had her arm around the back of Driver's neck.

"Well, it seems I found myself a family man."

"Dane…" I considered what Dane meant to do. In my mind's eye, I witnessed all kinds of horrors befalling Driver. Almost all of them included the officer's teeth. "What are you going to do?"

"I tell you what *you're* going to do," Dane said through the hole that was Driver's gaping mouth.

"You're going to drive away like nothing ever happened. Me and Officer Driver are going to step back to his car and have a... let's call it a 'come to Jesus meeting.'"

Sven, visibly shaken, said, "Please, Dane. You don't have to do this. I'll drive better. I promise. Fifty-five, stay alive. That's me, from here to Virginia."

"Go on. I'm done here." Dane opened the door and got out of the car.

"You can't do this!" Sven yelled after him.

"Remember, I only need one of you. Drive, Sven... *or else*," Dane said through the open driver's window. "Next time, maybe you'll think first before you act all foolish. Go on. My Melissa's waiting for you." Dane turned and walked Driver toward the rear of the car.

Sven's eyes leaked thick tears. They ran down his face, leaving snail-trails. "He can't, Ella. He can't."

"He can do whatever he wants, Sven." I saw Helena in that photograph, youthful and happy. Imagining her mother kneeling to give Helena the news about her father made my throat tighten. "We better get going like he said."

Sven stalled, his hand braced on the gear shift, and I looked into the side mirror. The officer's gun was out of its holster. Holding the pistol by the barrel, Driver began smashing the butt of the gun into his face. In the brake lights of our car, I could see dots, first red, then blue, falling from Driver's mouth onto the roadside. Officer Driver fell back onto the hood of the patrol car, stuck the barrel of the gun in his mouth, and blew his brains out.

Dane stepped out of Driver, leaving the officer's corpse to rest on the hood.

I watched Dane squat in the blue and red swirling lights. He began picking up teeth, one by one.

"What have I done?" Sven said, his voice clogged with emotion.

"Just go before Dane comes back."

Sven croaked, "That man had a family. People he cared for... people that cared for him back."

It seemed Sven and I had switched roles. He'd grown some humanity while I'd become colder. I said, "So did I. Those don't seem to last long. Not happy ones, anyway."

TWENTY-SIX

PHIL AND I MET OUTSIDE a George Strait concert in Denver on April 15, 1982. I wasn't a fan of the country bard, but I'd won the tickets after answering a question from one of the local radio stations and wasn't going to waste my prize. I'd called in to win the KISS tickets the station was giving away in tandem with the Strait tickets. The caller before me snatched up the KISS seats, so I was stuck with Strait. In my mind, at least I was getting out of the house.

I was in my last year of nursing school and living in a dorm room with a staunch Republican girl I called Smiley. She'd told me her name, but that didn't matter. Smiley fit her much better. The girl never smiled. I'd always been a fan of the ironic. Though Smiley didn't come with me, she became the reason Phil and I started talking in the first place.

Strait played at the Ogden Theater that year, and aside from the tickets the radio station gave away, the venue was sold out. Smiley dropped me off because I didn't have a car. Normally, I took the bus everywhere, but the transit system didn't run after seven o'clock, and the concert started at eight thirty. That night, Smiley wore a Reagan T-shirt, nothing more than the aged actor's face in white upon black cotton, the year

1980 in red below the president's jaw. Reagan had won the election, so there was no reason for Smiley to keep wearing the shirt. Perhaps it was fate.

Standing in line, I noticed two guys about my age milling through the crowd, trying to buy tickets off people. One of the guys was Hispanic. His eyebrows had grown beyond hope of control. Those things looked like caterpillars filled with ink. The second of the ticket-seekers was handsome by my standards, but what caught my eye was the T-shirt he wore. Smiley would have been proud. Reagan's bloodless face stared back at me from the second guy's chest.

I waved them over, and the handsome one came jogging up to me. The Spanish guy seemed not to have seen my beckoning hand.

"Yeah? You got tickets?" the guy asked.

I had my extra ticket in my purse, tucked into the cellophane of my cigarette pack, but I had no inclination to offer it for sale. I could have been arrested for scalping tickets.

"Well, I called you over to say my roommate has a shirt like that, but—"

"This damn thing? This ain't mine, lady. My buddy over there burned all my clothes, and our tickets right along with them. He gave me this shirt."

So he wasn't Republican or at least didn't seem to be happy about having to wear his buddy's shirt.

I asked, "Why did he burn all your stuff?"

"He thought I'd been sleeping with his old lady."

"Old lady?"

"His girlfriend. Jorge drives with an MC. They call their women old ladies."

"An MC?" I asked.

204

"Biker gang, but not the violent type. They just hang out, drink beer, and ride their motorcycles."

I laughed. "Not in that order, I hope."

"Wouldn't know. I don't trust myself to ride a bicycle, much less a bike with an engine."

"Gotcha." Then for some reason, I added, "I have an extra ticket. I don't want to get in trouble by selling it to you, but I could give it to you. Then, if your friend finds a ticket, you two could—"

"Forget my friend, lady. You got a goddamn deal."

I supposed I honed in on him because he was the exact opposite of me. He was rough and foul-mouthed, whereas I was soft and polite. He made my stomach warm when he spoke. Blasphemy or not, Phil could make my legs vibrate with only his words.

When I handed Phil the ticket from my pack, he asked, "You mind if I hang around?"

"If you want."

"I reckon I could." He ran his hand through his thick brown hair and smiled.

I needed a change of panties after that. "If you don't want to, I—"

"Oh, I want to. May want to take you out afterward too, truth be told."

I giggled. Giggled like a school girl. "You're very forward."

"Better'n backwards, I suppose. Been called backwards all my life. Nice to finally be forward in something."

"Where are you from?"

"Warner Robins, Georgia. You?"

"Well Being."

"Well being… what?"

I laughed. "Well Being is the name of the town. It's a city here in Colorado, about twenty miles south of Denver."

"Don't guess I ever heard of it. Only twenty miles south, you say?"

"Yeah."

"So we could go back to your place if this night goes well enough."

I should have slapped him. Had I had the proper mindset at that moment, I would have. Instead of reddening his cheek with the palm of my hand, I just winked at the guy. I didn't know what had come over me, but I liked the supercharged sexual tension that hung between us like electric fog.

By the time we made it to the ticket taker's booth, Phil — he finally introduced himself — had one of my butt cheeks firmly cupped in one hand. The booth lady asked for our tickets, and Phil patted his pockets.

Feigning surprise, he said, "Must've left them at home."

I whispered, "What are you doing?"

"Hopefully you."

We never saw George Strait that night, nor any other time. Phil found his buddy and handed the guy both tickets. The Spanish dude gave me a knowing smile, high-fived Phil, and we were off.

Phil had a Chevy Silverado that shined like a diamond in the parking lot lights of the Ogden Theater. He opened the door for me like a gentleman before going around to his side and sliding behind the wheel of the truck.

Phil had his penis out before we even left the parking lot. I gave him directions to my hometown even though my mouth was full for the journey. My jaw was quite sore by the time we hit Well Being.

Smiley was absent when we arrived at the dorm. We snuck in well enough and didn't rouse anyone's attention. I thought I would feel cheap, but I didn't. Somehow, I knew Phil was the guy for me, the man I would end up spending the rest of my life with.

Up until Phil, I'd only ever performed fellatio on two other guys. I had it set in my mind that oral sex was always better than giving away my sacred nu-nu, as if my vagina was buried treasure awaiting the return of Blackbeard himself. Phil was the first to pillage my treasure. He worried about the tearing, the blood my virgin womanhood spilled, but even though it hurt, it hurt in a good way, so I asked for more. His fervor grew, and my first time, unlike so many other women I'd heard from, was ecstasy. Phil even cuddled with me afterward. Then, in the shower while we cleaned up, he promised to stay with me until he died.

Fairytales never told a more perfect story.

Phil and I saw each other every night for the next month. When I missed my period, I scheduled an appointment with my doctor. The test came back positive. I called Phil and told him he needed to come over, that we had to talk. When he got there, the poor guy told me he thought I was going to dump him. I showed him the dipstick with the positive readout, and he cried. And then he left without explanation.

One long hour passed. That sixty-minute section of my life might as well have been an eternity. Finally, someone knocked on my door, and when I opened it, Phil was on bended knee.

"Didn't have one on me, so I had to run out real quick. Sorry I didn't say nothin'."

I bit my lower lip as he opened the small black box in his palm.

He cleared his throat, tears still twinkling in his eyes. "I don't reckon you'd want to marry me, wouldya, Ella?"

I never did say yes. I tackled Phil into the hallway of the dorm and kissed him until my lips felt fit to bleed. The black box with the single diamond ring inside had skittered away during my linebacker impersonation. I pushed myself off of Phil, snatched up the box, ripped out the ring, and shoved it on the proper finger.

I asked, "When?"

Phil got up off the floor. "Right now seems good and proper. Your probate do weddings?"

"If they don't, I'll make them."

Phil laughed, his smile the prettiest thing I'd ever seen. "May be a shotgun wedding after all."

Probate, luckily for them, did do weddings. My parents were out of town, and Phil's lived in Georgia, so Smiley and Jorge were our witnesses. I didn't wear a white dress—not because I was no longer a virgin, nor because I was pregnant, but because I didn't have time to find one. I wore my nursing scrubs. I was due at Clinicals after the service. Phil wore a blue blazer over his Reagan T-shirt, which he said reminded him of the night we met.

Nine months later, putting our conception date right at the first night Phil had taken me, Dane arrived in the world. I remembered thinking Phil's smile when he'd proposed to me had been the most beautiful thing I'd ever seen. And it was. Until our baby boy was born.

TWENTY-SEVEN

WHEN SVEN AND I PASSED over the Kentucky state line, the clock on the Nissan's dash read four fifteen a.m. Sven had stopped crying somewhere around four hours ago, but he still sniffled every now and then. The bags under his eyes were heavy, as if he carried piles of asphalt in those satchels. I asked him if he'd like to chance me driving for a while, and the look he gave me in response could have pierced stone. I tried to tell Sven that I had a license but just wasn't in possession of it, so they could run me, and I'd come back clean. Hopefully.

Sven said, "Drop it," and I did as I was told. I remembered Dane had warned us against more lawbreaking. I felt foolish for attempting to talk Sven into me taking the wheel.

The sun came up and settled above us. Sven drove for five more hours. At the Elizabethtown exit, he finally pulled off the interstate. My tailbone was screaming, and my tummy was rumbling something fierce. We had lunch at an IHOP. Sven ate very little. I devoured a Texas omelet and four triangles of toast slathered in strawberry jelly and tabs of margarine.

And just like that, we were back on the road. I assumed Sven still warred over the death of Officer Driver. Sven remained silent, and I didn't bother him.

Anything I could have offered would have been tired platitudes that probably would have enraged or saddened him further. Hours later, we passed a sign that told us London, Kentucky, lay forty miles away.

Sven's grasp on the steering wheel tightened. "I have to call Brandon." He jerked his chin at the green sign. "He's from London. Funny how life reminds you of stuff."

I nodded, not knowing how else to respond.

"Sorry, but I have to use speaker phone. Don't want to get in an accident because I'm talking on the phone." Sven mostly kept his eyes on the road while dialing. I knew very little about smartphones, but I knew they had memories that held contact information. I wondered why Sven hadn't added his lover's number for an easier time.

After two rings, a female voice answered. "Hello?" The accent wasn't thick, but hovered in the distance of the words it spoke.

Sven responded, "Hey, Brandy."

"And where have you been, hon? I figured you'd moved on by now."

I could have sworn to Jesus that Brandon was a woman without thinking twice about upsetting the good Lord. He sounded perfectly genteel, so womanly in tone that I felt a bit jealous. When a man sounded more like a woman than I did, it was time to reevaluate. For the first time in my life, I thought maybe I should lay off the cigarettes.

"This new story has had me running in circles. I'm sorry, baby."

I cringed. I couldn't help it. No matter how long I was around Sven, I didn't think I could ever get used to hearing a man call another man "baby." But that was my problem, not Sven's, so I said nothing and hoped he hadn't seen my nose crinkle.

Brandon — or Brandy — said, "When do you think you'll be back this way? I have a show coming up at the Paramount."

Sven asked, "When?"

"Around the third. Can you make it? I need you to RSVP for the VIP section, ASAP."

Sven laughed, "So many acronyms, my love."

"And so little time." Brandy Brandon giggled.

"I… uh… I love you, Brandy."

"Aww, sweetie, I love you, too."

"I mean it." For some reason, Sven looked at me and smiled.

I thought about Phil and me, how we were before Dane's abuse began, and I smiled back. Yes, Phil and I had been happy like Sven and Brandy once upon a time. Though it didn't last long.

"I know you do. Me, too. Listen, Pudding, you come home soon. I have plans for us. Kisses." Brandy accentuated his sentence with a loud *muah* sound.

"Returned. If… *when* I make it home, we'll see that your plans are put into play."

"I heard that 'if,' *Mr. Gödel*." Brandy's voice became stern. I suddenly knew why Sven didn't like me calling him by his last name. Brandy added, "What's wrong?"

Sven gave me a sad look. "I've… gotten into some trouble, but I'm working my way out of it. Someone doesn't like a story I did way far back, and they've been… harassing me."

"Tell them you have a hormonal drag queen waiting in Chi-town for them if they're feeling froggy."

Sven laughed. "God, I miss you, Brandy."

"Returned. Now, come home to me, will you?"

211

"Soon, baby. Soon. Get that black dress ready, eh? The one I like so much."

"You have a deal. Hurry home." Brandy gave off another car-filling "Muah!" before terminating the call.

In the disquieting silence resulting from the absence of Brandy's voice, I wondered if I should ask the question on the tip of my tongue.

Sven answered without me having to voice my query. "I really do love him. Will we be together forever? Probably not, but I'd like to hope we will. He's a good man and a strong woman. He brightens my life."

I was on the verge of tears but wasn't a hundred percent sure why. I guessed I missed the good old days with Phil, the times my family had when violence didn't rule the day. Though those periods were few and far between, and well behind me, I clung to them. I asked, "Why do you call him Brandy when you talk to him? Why not Brandon?"

"Depends on who he is on any given day."

I snickered. I couldn't help it. "I get that he's a transvestite—is that even the right word?" Sven nodded, so I continued, "But you make it sound like he's two different people."

"Oh, Brandon *is* two different people. Brandy is warm and caring and a blast to be around. Brandon would be the one I couldn't spend the rest of my life with. When Brandon and I talk, what you heard rarely ever happens. Brandon is still in the closet, whereas Brandy busted out a long time ago, taking all her clothes with her."

I thought about Dane, my son, and Dane, the killer. I believed I knew exactly what Sven meant, and I told him so.

"We all have that side of us we hide, Ella. I'm not the cutthroat journalist that you have come to know over the years, but he is a part of me. I'm really a very nice guy. Deep down."

"I've seen it closer to the surface these past few days."

"Have you now?"

"Yes, in fact I have." I shifted in my seat to rest my flattened buttocks. I rolled onto my left hip and looked at Sven with fresh eyes. "You're a very nice man. I'm sorry that I only just came to know the better side of you."

"Likewise."

"Likewise? What do you mean by that? I'm always a lady, until, of course, someone calls me an ignorant mother. I think you can understand that."

Sven smirked. "Are you hungry?"

I decided to let him get away with changing the subject. "I could use something. You should be famished. You barely ate any of your pancakes this morning."

"I didn't feel like eating."

"And you do now?"

"After talking to Brandy? Yeah, I kind of do."

I smiled, and Sven gave me one of his own. We had what I liked to call *a moment*. But somewhere in the back of my mind, I had to wonder… *where's Dane?*

We stopped in Hazard, Kentucky, the next city we came to after leaving London behind. Sven found a Fisher's fast-food restaurant on South Main Street after crinkling his nose as we passed another pizza place.

Though the thin redhead behind the counter said there would be a small wait on the fish while it cooked, my platter didn't hold one hot item. Sven's fish, however, steamed in mockery of my own. I figured mine had been from the previous batch. I thought, *leftovers, how nice.*

A thought materialized out of nowhere, and I felt the niggling need to ask Sven, "What did you eat while you were trapped in that hotel back in Well Being?"

"Chinese delivery. They would show up unannounced. I guess Dane called them. Who really knows, huh? He'd let me answer the door, but one time"—Sven took a bite of his fish, chewed and swallowed—"I tried to put my hand in the door to stop it from closing after the delivery girl left, and I about lost all the fingers on my right hand."

"Ouch."

"Yeah. You got that right."

The professional veneer he'd always showcased melted away, and Sven Gödel was just another guy seated across from me, enjoying a meal. The stream of questions abated, and we talked about life and family. Sven made no mention of me having been a bad mother, and I didn't call him on his out-of-line journalistic approach. Somehow, over the course of two days, we'd become friends.

When we finished eating, we commenced our journey into Virginia. As we crossed the state line, a heavy weight settled on my chest. I had no idea what to expect, but it would seem that our trek was coming to a close.

The last time we'd seen Dane was with Officer Driver, when Dane had told us through the officer's mouth that he had better things to do other than constantly *rescuing* us. Yet, something haunted me that I hadn't thought of before crossing over into Virginia.

What other things did Dane have to do? What gears was he setting into motion? What was his endgame?

Questions spilled out of my head, down the bridge of my nose, and over my breasts. I was covered in inquiries without a single answer in sight. I had become Sven, trying to interview myself and getting turned down at every juncture. After all, I had no answers. I hunted for explanations, but as we drove into yet another state, they continued to elude me.

I hadn't been paying much attention to signs and roads, nor had I even noticed many junctions, but as we came to Wytheville, Virginia, a hot coal began to burn in my gut. My head started pounding. There was no build-up. First, I didn't have a headache, then suddenly, I had a screaming migraine that squinted my eyes and threatened to paint the inside of the Nissan pink with brain matter.

Sven must have seen me struggling, because he asked, "You all right?"

I tried to answer, but all that came out was a pain-filled moan. I sounded like Phil rattling during his final breaths. It occurred to me that Dane had found a way into my skull and saw fit to burst right out of it by any means necessary.

"Ella?"

"Yarb?" was the sound that came out of me.

"Ella, look." Sven's voice didn't sound concerned anymore. Instead, his tone had a sour note, as if he was mad at me or something.

"I can't."

"You're gonna want to see this." Sven slowed the Nissan.

I tucked my head between my knees. "What is it?"

"What was the name of Dane's doctor?"

"I don't remember, but I could use one right now. Why?"

"Yeah, I forgot too, but it was Morrow… wasn't it?"

"Maybe. I don't know. My gosh-darned head is about to explode!"

"Before it does, I suggest you look up."

"Dang it! What?" I raised my head.

I wanted to be mad, furious at Sven for having made me open my eyes to the blinding sun that was so far behind us by then that the day had taken on a purple quality, but I couldn't. Sven was pointing, but I could see the sign just fine. I couldn't have missed it… well, unless my head actually did explode.

The red billboard had yellow lettering advertising a discount tire outlet. The name of the store was Doc Morrow's Tire And Tread. The subtitle read: Don't Wait 'Til Tomorrow To Call Doc Morrow. His Wheels Are A Steal!

I managed to say, "Can't be the same guy."

"Why not?" Sven accelerated and caught the off ramp.

"You saw the video. You heard Dane say the man was a therapist. Dane met Melissa there. She wanted to stop smoking. Remember?"

"In my town, everybody has their fingers in a multitude of pots. What's to say Doc Morrow's real passion isn't tires? Maybe Mommy and Daddy Morrow thought ol' Doc should be a head-shrinker. It's worth a shot. And Dane?" Sven looked around the car as if making sure my son could hear him in whatever astral plane Dane currently resided. "This is just a detour, buddy. No shenanigans, eh?"

No answer.

216

The closer we came to Doc Morrow's Tires and Treads, the more my headache eddied away. I was thankful, but not stupid enough to believe that it was simple coincidence. Every time Dane had appeared, I'd received some kind of throbbing in my skull. Whatever he was doing, he was making noisy work of my head.

Doc Morrow's establishment was directly off the interstate. The building, a long rectangle with four work bays big enough to house semis, was painted red at the bottom, then white, and finally blue. An American flag hung limp against the pole jutting from the side of Doc Morrow's roadside sign. The plastic letters slid into the signage read: We Will Never Forget 9/11. Seemed the owner was a bit patriotic. I made no assumptions as to why his sign still hearkened back to a tragedy more than twelve years prior.

Sven pulled into the parking lot on the left end of the building. "Should we have a plan?"

I rubbed my temples, though my headache had pretty much fled. "Ask questions."

"Nothing more? Should we take the gun?"

"What for? You think Doc Morrow is going to be packing heat? Calm down. We're just here to... inquire."

"Is that why we're here?"

"Look, *you* pulled off the interstate. *You* brought us here."

"Okay." Sven took a deep breath and sighed with his exhale. "Let's get this over with."

Sven and I opened our respective doors at the same time. We squeezed through a row of cars to reach the main walkway that wrapped around the building. I stepped up on the curb, approached the front doors, and went inside with Sven close behind me.

The room contained metal chairs and plastic tables, no doubt set up for people while they waited for their cars to be finished. At the back was a counter—red, white, and blue, just like everything else that surrounded me. Behind the patriotic podium stood a man with fading red hair and silver sideburns that reminded me of Elvis just before the King of Rock left our world by way of a commode and a fistful of medication. The guy's name was Ted, or so the white patch on his blue coveralls would have us believe.

I didn't know how else to start, so I asked, "Is Doc Morrow here?" as I went to the counter.

"That'd be me." The old man smiled. I saw how old he was then, in that smile. The wrinkles in his crow's feet numbered in the double digits. His grin looked as if it took all the strength he had left to lift the baggy, wrinkly sacks that had been cheeks once upon a time. I wondered how long it would be before I looked like Ted, or Doc Morrow, or whoever this guy was.

"Your name badge says you're Ted."

"Sh," he hissed jovially. "Don't spread my secret 'round. But honestly, folks"—he nodded at Sven—"I'm Doc Morrow if I'm a day old. My father called me Doc 'cause o' his name being Ted and all. You looking for tires? Got a sale on Bridgestones this month."

"We're actually just looking for you." I was a bit surprised that Sven was letting me do all the talking.

"Eh? Little old me? What makes me so important as to have a fine-looking woman like you knocking on my door?" He smiled wider, and those empty sacks he called cheeks touched his eyeballs.

"Do you remember a Dane Peters?"

Old Doc Morrow's cheeks crashed with all the subtlety of an unbalanced toddler failing to take its first steps. "And who's asking?"

Sven cut in, sounding incredulous, "So you remember him?"

"I asked who was asking."

I debated a moment on how much to reveal, then said, "I'm Dane's mother. Can I ask you a few questions?"

Doc Morrow looked both Sven and me over before walking to the door behind him. He wrenched it open and hollered, "Luther!" through the crack.

Ten seconds later, a short Hispanic man came through the door. "Yes, boss?"

Doc said, "Watch the counter. Come get me if someone shows up wanting service." And then, as if in afterthought, he added, "Please don't touch the till."

"Can do, boss."

Doc waved at Sven and me. "Follow me."

A hallway sat to the left, and Doc Morrow led us in that direction. He turned into the corridor and stepped into the first door on the right. The office was small, much too cramped for the three of us, but after Doc had me sit in the aluminum-armed plastic chair across from him and Sven leaned against the door after it was closed, the space seemed bigger somehow.

"You police?" Doc asked.

"No. I told you—"

"You'd tell me anything if'n you were five-oh. Whether you're cops or not, don't really matter. I never did anything wrong." Doc leaned back in the leather chair behind the small desk and stuffed his hands into the bib pockets of his coveralls. "I figured someone would come one o' these years. Didn't think it would be

Momma." Doc said it just like that, too. Not *Dane's momma*. Just Momma. "I guess you're wantin' to know that he worked here after he left you and that husband of yours."

"He talked about Phil?" I asked.

"Of course he did. Told me during his first interview. You know your boy hitchhiked all the way out here 'cause he had no place else to go? Nowhere else to turn? Huh? You know that?" Doc didn't seem angry, more disappointed than anything.

When I didn't answer right away, Doc said, "Well, he did. He come strolling up through the bay, nothing on him but his clothes, smellin' like sewer riptide on a hot July afternoon, askin' me for a job while I worked on somebody or another's car."

Sven asked, "And you hired him? Just like that?"

Doc nodded.

"Wait," I said. "Dane didn't have a driver's license back then. Phil wouldn't let him."

"I helped him get it. When he got his temp, I copied it and put it in his folder. I was the one got him the job at East-Western, too, after he completed his CDL training through some night school. I let him stay in the guest house out back of my place. He paid rent and was decent enough to strangers. Never had a complaint out of him. He wasn't with me but a year, though. He moved on, and I never heard from him again."

I turned to Sven. "None of this makes any sense. What about Melissa? Dane said he met her in a waiting room. She was here to stop smoking."

"Could very well have been," Doc Morrow said. "I used to run a smoking cessation group. All kinds came through my doors here looking for help. Twenty years without a cancer stick, myself."

I slumped back in my chair, not believing what I was hearing. If what Doc Morrow said was true, Dane had never sought out help, had never done anything to curb his murderous appetite.

Sven asked, "What about what you told him? Something about teeth. Ella? Help me out here. What about the teeth?"

Doc shook his head. "The teeth would lead him home. Yeah, I remember it. Don't think I ain't been kicking myself ever since, either. I done heard what he did to those people. What'd they call him all over the news? The Rest Stop Dentist? Yeah, that was it. I've been beating my head in about it for nigh on three years. Ever since they caught him, anyway."

"But why?" I asked. "Why would you say anything like that to someone?"

Doc Morrow met my eyes. I saw sadness, but there was anger there, too, just behind the sorrow. "He told me what your husband did to him. Knocked that boy's teeth outta his head… *twice*. I'd ask you if it were true, but I can see in your eyes that it is. I told him if he were ever gonna find any peace, he would have to learn to deal with that memory in his own way. He needed to find peace before he went off and hurt someone. I told him I thought that his whole big issue started with him losing his teeth. If he found that memory and got rid of it, tossed that recollection down the old crapper, he might get to feeling better. He actually said those words, not me. He said something like, 'So the teeth'll lead me home?' and my dumb ass said yes. But don't you go blaming me for your damaged son, Mrs. Peters. *You* screwed him up. You and your craptastic hubby sent that boy over the edge before he ever laid eyes on me."

Dane flickered into reality, perched atop Doc's desk like a crow on a highline. "You know… he's got a point."

Doc yelled, "What the Jesus jumped-up Christ is this shit?"

Dane said, "Be with ya in a sec, Doc."

I scooted my chair back as far as it would go, bumping hard into the wall behind me. Sven, like the hero he was, cowered in the corner, shaking. I couldn't really blame Sven for trying to climb into the walls. The room was already claustrophobic, but now there was a live viper in our midst.

"All this, Momma,"—Dane gestured at the surrounding room—"never had to happen."

I tried to remain calm. "We're going to see Melissa. There's no reason to be angry."

"Oh, you don't have a say in the matter. But I wasn't talking about the here and now. I was talking about me meeting Doc Morrow in the first place. If you woulda just stood up for me, if you woulda let us be a happy family, none of this would have ever happened. You realize that, right? That this was all your fault? Yours alone?"

"Is that what you want, Dane? For me to apologize for being weak? Fine, I'm sorry. I've always been sorry." The tears came. I was as powerless as I was terrified of my own son. "I'm so sorry. I'm sorry I didn't stop him. I'm sorry I failed you." I reached for his hand, but my own passed right through his. The air around me grew so cold I could see my breath.

"You'll get the chance to make it up to me, Momma."

I remained a blubbering mess, but I managed to ask, "What can I do? I can't turn back time."

"You'll see. You go on. Find my Melissa. Leave ol' Doc Morrow alone. You heard what I wanted you to hear. You can go now."

And just like that, Dane was gone.

I smelled poop heavy on the air. When Doc Morrow stood, I heard a squelching sound coming from the rear of his coveralls.

"What the flaming hell was that? You folks messin' with me?"

I pulled Sven out of the way of the door and dragged him out into the hallway, not unlike how he'd pulled me out of my house two days earlier.

"Ella," Sven groaned, "I-I don't think I can do this anymore. I'm sure I can't."

"You don't have any other choice, remember?"

Unlike me, Sven was strong enough to pull away. When I turned around, he was clutching the wall, trying to climb it as if he were Spider-Man.

"I can't!" he wailed.

Doc Morrow came out of his office. He ignored us and shuffled farther down the hallway, hopefully to a restroom, as the back of his coveralls were heavy and beginning to brown.

"Don't give up on me, Sven."

Sven swatted at my hands as I tried to approach him. "Don't touch me. Just go away. I'm done." He dug in his pocket and came out with the car keys. He threw them at me. "Go!"

I let them bounce off my stomach and fall to the floor. "Sven… please…"

"No! He wants to kill you… kill *us*. Don't you get that? You'll find this Melissa, and he'll possess her and have her kill you. Dead, Ella! Dead! I'm not going to watch someone else die. Let him have what he wants. If you're smart, you'll kill yourself and be done with it!"

"Don't... don't talk like that." Tears felt like molten steel on my cheeks. I couldn't stand anymore. I dropped to my knees and wept into my hands.

We'd come so far, and now Sven was lost. He made indistinguishable grunting noises as he either slammed his fists or himself into the wall of the hallway.

Not until Sven said, "Ella... help," did I look up.

His face was slack, his eyes dull, as he glared at me. Officer Driver's vacant gaze flitted into my vision.

I let out a shuddering, feeble breath. "No..."

"He's coming, Momma," Dane said through Sven's lips. "Whether the sissy likes it or not."

Dane had gotten better. Sven's mouth worked properly, not at all like Driver's loose hole of a mouth. Dane even sounded like Sven. It wasn't perfect, but it was close.

Sven took a shambling step forward, then another. He bent and picked up the car keys. The flesh puppet seized my wrist and yanked me up off the floor.

"License or not, you're gonna have to drive." Dane, or Sven, or *whoever*, handed me the keys. "My Melissa's waiting."

TWENTY-EIGHT

FBI SPECIAL AGENT CARMINE ANDREWS caught Dane. Well, he was accredited with the arrest anyway. A seasoned member of Quantico's best, Agent Andrews was a pillar of a man. I saw his picture in the newspaper and once on TV, then he simply fell off the radar. A reporter with CNN said that Andrews had retired, that having caught Dane, the man had finally capped his career. My son had been his final performance.

Andrews had been photographed leading Dane away in handcuffs, but the reality of the situation was that Dane had been apprehended due to a joint operation between local Virginian authorities and the Federal Bureau of Investigation. After receiving an anonymous tip that the Rest Stop Dentist would be making a jaunt into Roanoke, Virginia, Andrews had led the coup against Dane. The proper personnel were set up at rest areas, and agents dressed as attendants laid in wait for a white Peterbilt with an East-Western logo on its doors.

Dane pulled into the parking lot on his way into Virginia, killed the engine, and sat waiting for the proper time and person to strike. Around midnight, a middle-aged man—Andrews—pulled into the all but empty rest area. Andrews had been informed that Dane was at the location by the agent hidden inside the dimly lit welcome center. Dane didn't realize he was being watched, or so I assumed. I couldn't think of any reason why he would have stayed if he'd known he had a surveillance team on his tail.

Andrews went into the men's room, and Dane got out of his truck. Dane might have left that restroom unscathed if not for the fact that he'd brought a hatchet to the party, an implement with which he most likely planned to brain Agent Andrews.

Through ear-piece communication, the agent inside the welcome building radioed to Andrews that Dane was on his way. When Dane walked through the restroom doors, Andrews drew. Dane tried to charge the man and caught a bullet in the shoulder for his troubles.

After that, they searched his cab and found that copy of *A Christmas Carol*, the Asian porno movies, and Dane's collection of teeth.

All those facts came from regurgitated courtroom testimonies from officers and agents on site at the time of Dane's capture. The photo of Carmine Andrews leading Dane away in cuffs came from none other than Sven Gödel. Sven had been invited to the soirée by Andrews to document the capture of my son. Sven just happened to bring a camera along. Good times were had. It was a party of sorts.

The world was finally safe from the threat of the Rest Stop Dentist, and I eventually watched my son die.

TWENTY-NINE

THE SVEN BOT SAT IN the passenger seat while I drove. I started referring to him in my mind as Sven Bot so as not to confuse myself any further. He wasn't Sven, couldn't really be called Dane, either, so Sven Bot he was. I imagined Dane inside Sven's head, pulling levers to make Sven's body work, like some automaton. Yes, Sven Bot was apt.

I stayed five miles per hour under the posted interstate speed limit. The trip into Roanoke took an hour and forty-five minutes because of it. By the time I hit the ramp, night had fallen. I turned off of I-81 and onto I-581, passing the Roanoke Airport on the way into the middle of the city. I followed the GPS onto surface streets. I spotted a Bojangle's Fried Chicken and found myself suddenly very hungry. My lunch of cold fish had long since worn off, but I didn't think Sven Bot wanted to hear that, so I kept my grumbling gut to myself.

I pulled onto West Ninth Street and followed it until it became East Ninth. I started watching for an apartment complex, but didn't see one. According to Melissa Dugan's address, she lived in apartment ten of something.

"Just up there." Sven pointed at a motel with a sign stating weekly rates were available. Dane sounded exactly like Sven. My stomach began to churn until it hurt, hunger and fear making me queasy.

The motel was shaped like an upside-down L. The building housing the office had an awning facing the street. A row of shrubbery hid the entirety of the parking area, so I couldn't see the door numbers.

I maneuvered the Nissan through the entrance of the lot, past the line of shrubs. At the elbow of the L, I did a brief door count without pulling ahead any farther. Noticing four police cars sitting between what looked like rooms eight through twelve, I eased my foot onto the brake and cut to the left, gliding under the awning. At the front doors of the office, out of sight of the cruisers, I pushed down on the brake, and the Nissan lurched to a sudden stop. Sven Bot jerked forward, rapping his forehead on the dash. He should have been wearing his seat belt. No sound of pain came from Sven Bot. Dane made him look at me with an angry face. I didn't like that Dane had control over Sven's facial features. Things just seemed to be getting worse all the time.

To my right was a glass-fronted building with hours of operation on the door. Beyond the entrance, a dark-skinned man with Arab features, no doubt the desk clerk, busied himself at a computer screen.

Sven Bot said, "What are you doing, Momma?"

"Did you see the cops?"

"I can handle them. Pull back around."

"No." I didn't know where my sudden courage came from.

"No?"

"I mean…" I tried to breathe so I could form words, but no air would come. What did come out came in a heated rush. "They'll leave eventually, then you can do what you want. No reason to kill any more people, Dane, please."

"You really think I'm worried about body counts?"

"Please. You'll have your way. Just not here. Not now. Look at it this way: You can't control more than one person at a time, right?" I didn't wait for Sven Bot to answer. "What if Melissa gets hurt? What then? You didn't come all this way to see her dead or injured, right?"

"No." Dane was even taking on Sven's cool, professional demeanor.

I wondered how long it would be before I questioned whether or not my son was still inside the journalist. My hands grew sweaty on the steering wheel. The idea of not being able to tell the difference anymore terrified me.

Sven Bot seemed to be thinking something over. "Okay. Pull out and make a right. Go the direction you were headed before you pulled in."

I said, "Hang on," as I popped open my door.

Sven Bot growled, "Where do you think you're going?"

I pointed in the direction of the cruisers I couldn't see anymore. "If they notice me just pulling out of here without so much as going inside, they're bound to follow us."

Sven Bot set a cold glare on me. "Go on. You take too long, and I make pudding of Sven's brain."

I grimaced. I didn't think Dane was exaggerating one iota. I could almost see the pink soup as it dribbled from Sven's ears. "I'll be back. Don't worry about that, Dane."

Of course, I knew why the police were there, but that didn't lessen my surprise. No doubt someone had found Stanley dead in my foyer, so they would also have searched my house. The responding officers would have found Melissa Dugan's information hanging from the fridge. That info might have been passed along to Roanoke's finest, and there they were, wanting to know of Melissa's association with the woman who'd left a dead body back in Well Being, Colorado. I was risking arrest, or hoping for it, by getting out of that car, but I'd seen no officers stationed outside the rooms or patrolling the grounds. The makeshift apartments didn't look overly large, so I imagined the police were all in Melissa's place, squeezed together like fish steaks.

I had a plan, though. If only I could manage to pull it off.

I got out and went to the door of the registration office. *Für Elise* bell chimes greeted me when I opened the door. The brown-skinned man behind the counter had moved away from the computer terminal and was looking down, possibly doing paperwork. A hand holding a pencil came into view. His index finger jutted out, as if telling me to wait a second.

Confirming my assumption, he said, "Be right with you."

I hovered at the door, not knowing how else to proceed. I craned my neck and looked out at Sven Bot in the Nissan. No one else was outside. My luck was in a holding pattern of sorts.

"Oh, dear," the desk clerk proclaimed.

I turned back around just as he put a phone receiver to his ear. His eyes were wide, maniacal, like a zoot-suit-adorned wolf in one of those old cartoons, having just spotted a feisty little number in a red dress.

I took the space between me and the desk in five long strides. The man moved two steps back, bumping into the wall behind him. The cord of the phone was plenty long and dangled between him and the desk like an expansion bridge. I reached over the desk, found the phone's base, and shoved my thumb onto the catch, terminating the call.

"Oh, dear," he repeated. He reminded me of Talia, all "Dear, dear, deary!"

"Who were you calling?"

"They... um... they're looking for you."

I located his name tag. "Listen, Rodney—*Rodney*?— whatever, listen. I assume they showed you my picture, right?"

He nodded in quick, jerking movements that shook his thin frame.

"Well, I'm not the problem. You wouldn't believe me if I tried to explain, but I want you to know, that man"—I pointed behind me at Sven Bot in the passenger seat of the Nissan—"has me held captive. I need you to pass a message on to the police. Can you do that?"

He never stopped nodding. I was afraid the poor man's neck might snap and his head would roll off onto the carpet.

"You tell them we came by, like they knew we would, and we saw them, the police, and that we're leaving town. We're on the run. You got that? You can tell them that, right? You'd save my life if you did. Understand? You'd save my life."

"He's going to kill you?" At first, I thought Rodney was telling me, but then I realized he was asking me a question.

"Yes. He very well may kill me, especially if you don't tell them that they need to look somewhere else for us. Okay?"

"How do I know you're not lying?"

I sighed in frustration. "You… you don't, all right? But could you look at your wife—"

"I'm not married."

"Fine, your girlfriend?"

He started nodding again.

"Good. Could you look at your girlfriend again, knowing you helped kill some poor woman by not passing along a simple message?"

I was happy as a pig in refuse when Rodney stopped nodding and began shaking his head.

He said, "That Dugan woman is a good girl. Always pays on time. She won't be hurt?"

"Not if you pass along my message." I heard the Nissan's car door slam and realized I was out of time. That was good, though. Sven Bot would play to my advantage.

When I turned around, Sven Bot stood in the doorway, *Für Elise* announcing his arrival. He had Sven's gun gripped firmly in his fist and aimed at me.

Sven Bot roared, "Move!" and the windows actually shook with his voice.

I stood between Sven Bot and Rodney. Dane couldn't get a decent bead on the desk clerk. I waved my hands like a runway attendant signaling a plane not to land.

"No no no! You don't understand!" I yelled. "He's going to help the cops go away. You can have me. I'm all yours."

"I saw you pointing at me. What did you tell him?"

"That we're leaving."

"What else?"

I thought about my next words very carefully before saying, "And that the cops should come find me... *us*. That they should come find *us*."

Sven Bot glared at me. "Go out to the car."

"You're coming, too. I'm not going to let you kill this man."

Rodney chanted an incoherent prayer behind me. I caught one word in all the garbled sentences: Allah.

"He's scared. He's going to tell the police we left. Right, Rodney? You're going to tell them to come find us. Right? *Right*?"

"Yes, oh dear, yes! Please don't kill me."

Sven Bot lowered the gun and walked outside. I was finally given a moment to work on my breathing. I couldn't believe I'd actually talked Dane out of killing Rodney. I didn't suspect that I held any sway over my dead son, but maybe he'd seen the error in his logic. If he'd killed Rodney, the police would be all over us like a groom mounting his bride on their wedding night.

On my way out, I told Rodney, "Please don't fail me."

He cringed. "I think I failed my pants."

With the desk clerk's possible lack of bladder and bowel control on my mind, I rejoined Sven Bot out in the car.

I followed Sven Bot's instructions, moving deeper into Roanoke. We came to a place called Happy's Flea Market, and Sven Bot told me to pull in. The sign had a yellow grinning face that reminded me of my old roommate, Smiley. Memories of her made me think of Phil, so I just stopped thinking, period. I didn't need any more crap floating to the surface. Not then. Not there.

The parking lot was filled with cars and trucks with some minivans and trailers thrown in for good measure. Each car's trunk or hatch was open, and in the case of trucks, the tailgates were down. I'd been to many places like Happy's. The parking area was used for people who didn't want to pay for building space inside but would no doubt be charged an admittance fee to sell their goods on the asphalt outside at a much cheaper rate than renting a cubicle.

I drove through the aisles at an idle pace, surveying the goods being sold. Some individuals had erected foldaway tables behind their vehicles, where everything from knickknacks to power tools was on display. Potential customers and haggling salespersons busied themselves in the crowd, seemingly ignoring our presence. They probably had drive-bys all the time, the flea market equivalent of window shopping.

At the rear of the parking area was a square brick building with glass double doors that lent entrance to the interior section of the flea market. A yellow banner hung just above it, the location's name printed in red letters.

I asked Sven Bot, "What are we doing here?"

"My Melissa works here. She'll be selling tomorrow. The people that work out here are allowed to leave their vehicles overnight, for a price. You'll pay the fee for a parking space, and then we'll go walk around town."

I sighed. "I'm tired, Dane."

"I'm not."

"Can't we get a hotel or something? I'm going to be of no use to you."

"You'll make it."

"Please?"

Sven Bot twisted in his seat, grabbed my throat, and squeezed until I saw black spots in my vision. The foot I had over the brake went stiff, and I stomped the pedal. Both of us swayed forward in our seats.

Sven Bot hissed in my ear, "You do not run this show, Momma. No hotels. Besides, they'll be looking at hotels 'cause of your stunt back at my Melissa's place."

His grip loosened, and I melted into my seat, sucking wind. When I looked up, two women were gawking at us from beside an empty boat trailer. One shook her head but remained staring. The other looked away, making us no business of hers. I wanted to plead to them, but I knew there was nothing they could do. If I even motioned to them, Dane would make short work of the pair.

I brought myself back under control by rubbing the soreness out of my neck and focusing on my breathing. In through the nose, out through the mouth. I asked God for strength. I couldn't manage any more courage on my own. Finally, I asked, "You don't think they'll look here?"

"They don't know this car. They're looking for Sven's fancy car."

"How do you know that?"

Sven Bot beamed at me. "I have my ways. Park there." He pointed at an empty spot a little ways down from where I had stopped.

I pulled in between a maroon SUV with its hatch up, selling what looked like ceramic gnomes or maybe Santas, and a gray panel van with acoustic guitars hanging from hooks inside the inner compartment. I put the Nissan into park and killed the engine.

I didn't know what else to do, so I just sat there, trying to recollect Bible verses with strength as their main theme. Every single one eluded me. Instead of scripture, another thought came to mind. *God helps those who help themselves.*

I needed answers. Seated next to me was a direct contradiction to my faith. Dane should have been burning in a lake of fire, not out possessing people. Possession was touched upon many times in the Bible, but every chronicled occasion focused on demonic entities, not ghosts. Recalling a verse in Matthew 9 where a mute man spoke after a demon had been exorcised from him, I decided to consult the source of my questions.

Steeling myself, I asked, "How are you doing any of this, Dane? Why didn't you just… go to the other side? Why didn't you move on?"

Sven Bot looked around. He seemed to be thinking, and thinking hard at that. "I have things to take care of here. You'll find out soon."

"But how? I see you, I've seen you since just after you died, but I still don't believe in ghosts. I can't. I'm a Christian woman. You should either be in heaven… or Hell."

"Ever heard of astral projection?"

"Mystic crud. Yes, I have."

Sven Bot focused on me. The right eye went lazy, turned in to look at the nose. Dane fixed the malfunction, and both eyes met mine. "I read a great deal about astral projection in prison. I had nothing better to do. Meditation and all that jazz seemed a good waste of time. But what I found helped me come to grips with the fact that this world ends, but we don't. Not if we don't want to. I read up on chakras and different planes of existence, and all that stuff I thought, like you, was mumbo jumbo." The more Sven Bot spoke, the more of Dane came forth, as though he was forgetting who he was supposed to be. Sven's proper grammar and speech patterns were melting away.

Though I didn't believe Dane's explanation, I decided to press further. "So how did you manage to stay alive?"

"I projected myself. When they stuck them needles in me, I went to my valley. My valley is a pretty place, Momma. It has a creek where I fish. I go there when I need to think. My Melissa and my… and me. She's there with me, is what I was getting at."

"There's someone else there, isn't there? I heard you stutter."

"Not that you'd care, but yeah, there is."

"Who?"

"Don't be worrying about that. Get out. We got walking to be doing." Sven Bot grabbed the door handle and made to get out.

"It's your father, isn't it?"

Sven Bot came at me in a flash. Dead eyes, bereft of the life Dane had given them just moments before, bored into mine, melting my soul. "You don't ever speak to me about him!"

I cowered, pushing myself against my door as if I could just melt inside of it and be gone from the snarling monstrosity before me. "I'm… I'm sorry, Dane."

"I got all the sorry from you that I can mustard."

Incredulously, motherly, I said, "It's 'muster.'"

"Damn your mustard and your muster. Damn this whole stupid nonsense. I'm going to show you what should've happened. I'm going to make everything right, and you're going to be happy for once!"

I couldn't believe what I was hearing. "You… you want me to be… *happy*?"

"If it kills you, yes. And it very well may. Makes no difference to me. Now, get out."

Together, we left the Nissan.

Sven Bot found a man wearing a Happy's shirt. He paid the employee ten dollars for the spot we'd taken. After that, I followed Sven Bot across the road to an Arby's, my empty tummy growling in anticipation of roasty-beefy-goodness. We crossed the street during a break in traffic and jogged to the opposite sidewalk.

The autumnal air felt brisk on my face. The trees surrounding the restaurant, as sparse as they were there in the city limits, had begun changing colors, and I hoped it wouldn't be my final fall amongst the living, in either sense of the word. I almost didn't want to go inside the restaurant, but when I hesitated at the door, Sven Bot dragged me in by my wrist.

He ordered for me—a roast beef sandwich smothered in gelatinous foodstuffs with a side of curly fries. Sven Bot didn't eat. He only watched as I ravaged my dinner with gluttonous abandon. I felt bad for Sven. I had no way of knowing where within Sven Bot the journalist actually resided, but I hoped he couldn't feel the hunger pangs that must be gnawing at his insides.

Out of the wild blue yonder, Sven Bot said, "I miss eating. My Melissa used to make the best roast beef. She'd cook it all day long, kinda like you used to. We have it sometimes in my valley. We live in a little cottage by the creek. Did I tell you about the cottage, Momma?"

I was stuck stuffing my face, frozen with a handful of curly fries as they fought for entrance into a mouth that no longer worked. All I could think about was Sven, his words about the two sides to every human being since the dawn of man. The man that possessed Sven Bot was no longer my serial-killer son, but my baby boy, reminiscent and kindhearted. I shook my head, fries still blocking my ability to speak.

"Yeah, the cottage is nice. I come out of it one day, maybe two or three days after they filled me full of poison, and my Melissa was gone. She'd taken… she'd left without me." Sven Bot's eyes crossed, Dane suddenly unable to control them, or so it seemed. He looked so sad and goofy that I wanted to cry.

"So I went looking for them, Momma. I went looking, and I found that I weren't dead like I thought I was. Sure, they killed my body, but I… me… Dane weren't dead. I found my way back to my Melissa, here in Roanoke, but she couldn't see me. She just kept on going about life. I didn't know where else to turn. I didn't have nowhere else to go. I… I shoulda stayed dead. If I was ever dead. But then I got to thinking. Thinking about how I ended up in this whole damn mess to begin with. So's I went hunting Dad, but Dad were dead. The only one left was you. And I saw that I had to try and make up for what you let him do to me. I had to fix things before I could move on, if I'm ever going to move on. First, I need to see my Melissa, and I aim to use you two to make that happen. If she'll see me, maybe I can rest."

"Dane, hon, I'm—" I reached for Sven Bot's hands, touched the cold skin, and pulled away.

"El-Ella?" Sven's eyes were hazy, but they were Sven's. I could see the concern in his face.

"Is that… Sven?"

"Yuh-yeah…" Sven's eyes rolled back in his head, and he crumpled. Rolling out of his chair, his head hit the floor with a *smack*.

It never ceased to amaze me how uncaring the world was. Sven spilled out onto the floor, and not one person came to help. Sure, the folks behind the counter stared, but they didn't act. They seemed to be waiting for me to ask for assistance. I guessed that was for the best, given how we were essentially fugitives and all.

I slid out of my chair and kneeled beside Sven, who groaned and grumbled something I couldn't understand. "Sven? Sven, you okay?" I slapped him lightly on his cheeks until his eyes focused on mine.

"I'm hungry."

I let a rip of laughter fly from me. It was half relief and half anxiety. "You scared me to death."

"Food, muh… I need food. Then, we talk."

I reached into his pocket. "I'm not trying anything fresh, just gonna grab your wallet."

"You groping me is… is the least of my worries."

I helped Sven climb back into his chair, then I walked up to the counter and ordered him three one-dollar roast beef sandwiches. Two minutes later, I returned with his meal.

I said, "I'm sorry. I didn't think to ask if you wanted fries."

Shaking his head, Sven tore into his food, eating with the fervor of a man who'd just been given leave from a concentration camp. Halfway through his second sandwich, he ran to the restroom, where I assumed he threw up.

He came back to the table, wiping his mouth with a brown paper towel, and slid into his seat. "Guess I need to slow down."

"Where'd Dane go?"

"I don't know. I don't want to know. At least he's gone. It's scary being him, or him being me... or whatever happened."

"Do I need to fill you in?"

"No. I could hear everything. I could even see at times. You know how dreams feel? Like you know it's all happening, and you should have control, because it's your dream, but you can't seem to get things to go right?"

"I know all too well. That's been my life after Dane."

He laughed. "Yeah, I can see that." He nibbled at the other side of his half-finished sandwich.

"Calm down, big guy."

"I'm feeling better now. Much better."

I was about to settle in and become accustomed to having my friend back, but a thought stopped me dead. "You almost called me 'Momma.'"

"What? When?"

I felt my heart break in my chest. I was sick of the games. "While you were on the floor. God bless it, stop messing with me, Dane. For the love of God, I can't take this anymore."

Sven Bot was back, if he'd ever really left. He winked at me. "I'm getting better though, right? Oh well, time to go, Momma."

"You bastard."

"Such language. Sometimes, though, I wish I were one. A bastard, that is. Not having Dad around might have cured all my troubles. But only *you* could have made that happen."

Instead of sitting back down at the table, Sven Bot led me outside by my wrist. We walked, and we walked, then we walked some more. My legs gave out on me three times. Sven Bot would grab me up and drag me along until I caught my second wind. I was breaking; I could feel it. Dane's toying with me had cut something loose of its moorings. My brain collapsed on itself in a supernova that threatened to consume all reasonable thought.

I didn't take in my surroundings. We might have walked past the Egyptian pyramids, and I wouldn't have noticed. I did remember a comic book shop and a grocery store, but the rest was a blur.

Finally, Sven Bot led me back to the Nissan, where he allowed me to lie down in the back seat. "They come around at four in the morning. You got three hours to sleep. Then, we have our reunion."

I didn't want to know what Sven Bot meant. I only desired sleep, precious, mind-numbing, unfaltering, empty sleep. I dreamed of convicts wearing orange jumpsuits, perched on mountains of roast beef and urinating flames into the valley where I stood. A cottage burned. I went to the creek to collect water. I had a bucket, but the creek ran with yellow, processed cheese. I doubted the cheddar foodstuffs would put out the raging inferno.

All around me, a symphony of voices spewed forth from the giant, urinating prisoners. "The teeth'll lead me home!"

THIRTY

ONE MONTH PAST DANE'S DUE date, my doctor decided to induce me. Even after ten months inside me, my son seemed not to want to come into the world. Phil joked that maybe Dane was scared of the bright lights overhead in the delivery room, comparing our son to Punxsutawney Phil, the beloved Pennsylvanian groundhog who was perpetually frightened by his own shadow.

Phil remained stoic and smiling at my bedside, clutching my hand as my aged obstetrician administered the Pitocin that would expedite Dane's arrival. I cringed at the feeling of the doctor's cold, latex-clad fingers as they entered me to measure my cervix. Focusing on Phil's hand, I watched his nails turn white, deprived of blood flow.

My husband made no complaints about my vise-like grip, only petted my hair and kissed my forehead. "He'll be here soon, Ella. Our baby boy's coming."

Two hours later, I pushed a Buick through a doughnut hole. Dane came screaming into the world without having to be spanked into breathing. The doctor hefted my son up for me to see as a nurse handed Phil a pair of scissors. I didn't see Phil cut the cord. I was too enamored by what the two of us had created. Dane's ruddy face, wrinkled in effort, was the most beautiful sight I'd ever beheld. The doctor handed Dane off to a second nurse, who waited beside him with a receiving blanket opened like a catcher's mitt.

She toweled him off then laid him atop my chest. I wanted to hug and squeeze and kiss and scream, all at the same time. A heavy feeling had settled upon my heart, contentment wrapped in fear of the unknown.

Quite clearly, I saw Dane the toddler, stumbling around our home, falling over, picking himself back up, only to go tumbling down again. I witnessed his first bike ride without training wheels, his voice high and proud as he hollered, "Look, Momma! Look what I can do!" Phil taught the boy how to fish, thread worms, and cast practice lines, and all the while, Dane watched in wide-eyed amazement at his father's adept skills. Dane, standing at the head of our church, a tuxedo fitted elegantly to his chiseled form, smiled as his wife-to-be was led down the aisle to the tune of "Here Comes the Bride." Grandkids assaulted me, clambering up my body, fighting for sole attention, while Phil and Dane shared a beer in the kitchen.

All those visions came to me in an instant and were gone just as quickly. I focused on the baby in my arms, my little man so gorgeous and handsome that I knew every woman alive would soon be in trouble.

Soon after my imaginings left me, the same nurse who'd handed him to me took Dane from my arms. I protested, but she only smiled.

"He's gotta get cleaned up," she said. The nurse carried him over to a warming table. A nest of blankets had been arranged in the bottom of the heated bed. She carefully laid him down, and he cawed, much like an angry crow.

Phil approached the Plexiglas-sided table and reached into it. Dane, uncannily, latched onto his father's middle finger. Phil smiled so big and bold that it brought tears to my eyes.

Phil looked over to me, his own tears glistening on his cheeks. "That's it, then. We're a family, Ella. A real-life, honest-to-God family."

THIRTY-ONE

"GET UP!"

I rose with a start, sitting bolt upright in the back seat of the Nissan. It took me a few seconds to catch hold of my bearings. Outside the car, night, or early morning, welcomed me with a dark countenance. Roast-beef mountains and flaming cottages still haunted my vision. My stomach spoke to me, but I doubted breakfast would come that morning.

Rubbing my eyes, I asked, "What time is it?"

"Just after four. Everyone's showing up. We got to move," Sven Bot answered from the front seat. He popped open his door and got out.

I adjusted my neck in slow circles, sleep ebbing away with all the urgency of a snail traveling uphill. I leaned forward and opened the passenger-side rear door. I slid on my butt until my feet touched asphalt, then I stood up.

Surveying my surroundings, I took in the parking lot and the building that housed the main part of the flea market. Three people stood at the front doors, under the lights cast by the security lamps on either side of the Happy's sign: a bald man in jeans and a yellow T-shirt, a woman in her thirties, and seven-year-old Dane.

I did a double take. I had to rub my eyes again and collect myself. Dane resided in Sven Bot, so I doubted what I was seeing was real. Sure, Dane had said he could project himself, but the apparition my son had become was the projection. I didn't expect he could be in two places at once. The possible ramifications of that idea chilled my soul. I tried to assure myself that what I was seeing was just a trick Dane had pulled on my tired psyche.

A second woman strode across the parking lot toward the small group at the doors. None of them seemed to be paying attention to Sven Bot and me, more interested in welcoming the approaching woman. She was thin in the upper body but large in the rump. For all intents and purposes, she looked like an eggplant. Her purple blouse and black pants added to that simile.

Sven Bot, standing at the front of the Nissan, said, "Let's go."

I noticed the gun in his hand, and my gut grew cold. "What are you going to do?"

"Why didn't you ask this many questions while Dad was beating the hell out of me? Huh?"

Dane had a point. I shut up. I didn't have the energy any longer, and I didn't think I would be able to waylay another murder spree. I just wanted it to be over, and I hated myself for that.

The space between us and the four at the door wasn't more than fifty feet, but it felt like miles. As we went, Eggplant unlocked the door, reached in and flipped on some lights, then held the door open for the group of three to enter the building. The last one in was seven-year-old Dane.

Sven Bot raised the gun and blew off the top of Eggplant's head. I flinched, the sight of her exploding skull disgusting me, but not much else. I'd become desensitized by the trail of death Dane had left behind us. Screams poured from inside the building until Eggplant's slumping corpse pushed the door closed.

Sven Bot trotted over and retrieved the set of keys from Eggplant's loose grip. He then pushed the woman out of the way with a sweep of his foot and entered the building. I followed like a cow being led to slaughter, numb and praying the end of the whole mess would be quick and painless.

Another gunshot blasted me out of my thoughts, and I saw the front of the bald man's yellow shirt turn orange. He dropped to his knees in the atrium, clutching his chest and wheezing like a steam kettle, before falling face first onto the horrid green-and-red-checkered tile.

With Eggplant's keys, Sven Bot locked us all inside.

I had only a second to look around. Cubicles had been set up throughout the floor of the flea market's main building. The huge room looked as if it had once been a concert hall with wide-open floors to help with acoustics. Tables filled with bric-a-brac, knickknacks, tools, and electronic equipment covered almost every available space. The woman was running toward the back, dragging Child Dane by his hand.

"Where are you going, Mimi?" Sven Bot spoke lightly, almost tenderly.

The woman stopped. A mother's instinct would have kept her running—I thought I would have to save my own son—but a bullet to the back seemed a poor way to leave your child.

My own son…

I looked at Sven Bot… at Dane. He gazed at me with leaking eyes. His tears terrified me because I knew that look. It was a parent's pride.

"Momma, this is my Melissa. And that"—he pointed at the boy—"is your grandson, Phillip."

Phillip? I felt sick, confused, and shattered. Dane had named his son after his father. My brain reeled, stealing away any rational thought. I was shaking my head. I couldn't stop. Just like that Arab desk clerk nodding, I simply couldn't stop.

Sven Bot's gaze left mine, and he trained the gun on Melissa. "Come here, Mimi."

She wasn't an overall pretty woman. She looked rather plain, no makeup, her hair a rat's nest. Her clothes, definitely either old or second-hand purchases, made her look homely. I remembered where she lived, in that pay-by-week motel. Dane had gone for the antithesis of me, just as he'd said in Sven's video. Sure, we'd had our financial troubles while he was growing up, but we never let on. To Dane, we were a well-off family, secure and managed. Well, managed aside from the torture Phil laid upon him. Even Phillip, who was most definitely my son's child, looked poor and hungry. I felt a pang in my heart for that poverty-stricken family of two. I imagined what Melissa must have gone through and wondered which was worse: money and abuse, or needy and unharmed.

Phillip was crying, but Melissa stood steady.

"I said, come here, Mimi," Sven Bot repeated.

Melissa hollered across the forty-some-odd-feet between us, "I'm sorry, all right? I never thought you would find out!"

She seemed to be talking to me. Sven Bot glanced my way, a look on his face that said he thought the same thing.

Looking back at Melissa, he smiled wide. "No need to be sorry. I'm back, Mimi." He seemed to have forgotten the skin that he wore. Melissa didn't see Dane; she saw his puppet, Sven.

"You were never supposed to find out. Please, don't hurt us!" That comment made me look back at Melissa and really focus on her. Her words were in English, but they were still a jumbled-up puzzle. I had the box and the diagram, but I couldn't put all the pieces together.

Melissa blubbered, "I'm so sorry, Ella."

I asked, "Why are you sorry? What did you ever do to me?"

"I didn't know what else to do, so I called the cops."

My mind crumpled under the sheer weight of my confusion. How could she have known I was coming to see her, and even if she did, why did she expect me to harm her? I'd assumed the officers at the motel had been sent there because of the contact information on my fridge. Even the desk clerk, Rodney, had said they'd passed around my picture.

Melissa moved Phillip behind her. "All I meant to do was clean out his truck for him. Then I found those teeth. I... I got scared. I'm sorry they killed your son!"

Oh, God! This isn't good. This isn't good at all. The anonymous caller had been Melissa Dugan—Dane's Melissa... Mimi. *God, save us all.* Dane's family reunion had been destroyed; whatever he'd hoped to accomplish was flushed down the drain.

I twisted my neck, slowly, and the bull that was Sven Bot flared his nostrils.

Dane raged, "You did *what*?"

Melissa yelled, "Phillip, run! Don't look back!"

Dane stepped right out of Sven Bot like a man striding through a door, just as he had left Talia and Officer Driver.

Melissa screamed. So did I. I had no idea why I should be so surprised, but I was.

Dane's voice was a thundering, booming thing. "You turned me in? You?" His head snapped in my direction. "Why couldn't I find that in your head? Where were you hiding it?"

I took a step back. "Dane... Dane, I didn't know." I drew up my arms to protect myself, shielding my face in the process. When nothing came, I lowered my defenses.

Dane was gone.

Many things happened in the briefest instant. Sven seemed to melt to his knees in one slow motion. The barrel of the gun clacked against the red and green tile. He looked like a depressed monkey, his arms seeming longer than his legs in his kneeling position. He looked up at me, and I saw the death in those eyes. In my peripheral vision, I saw Dane, pulsing with an eerie darkness like thrown shadows, choking Melissa in the middle of the aisle between the tables. Phillip must have taken his mother's advice, for there was no sign of the boy.

Sven's voice drew my attention. I focused on my broken friend. His voice was dry and cracked more than once when he spoke. "He wants me to be a father. I'm no father. I don't wanna be... Daddy."

Sven put the gun to the side of head.

I moaned, "No…"

Sven's eyes, those windows to the soul, told me he was already far past gone, barren, and bereft of any will to go on. "The teeth will lead you home, Ella. Buh-bye now."

I heard the gunshot, but averted my eyes in time so as not to see the damage done by the large-caliber round when it passed through Sven's snapped mind.

Sven's death rocked me, but his final words, different from how Dane had said them, gave me a thought. A horrid, nasty idea burrowed in my psyche, planted eggs, and spawned, all in a matter of milliseconds.

Praying, *Please, God, let Sven be right*, I went in search of the tool that would lead Dane off into eternity. Hopefully one of flame.

Tools. I had seen tables with tools when I first came into the flea market. I had to find that table again. Melissa wouldn't last long, then poor, destitute Phillip would no longer just be impoverished; he'd be an impoverished orphan. I couldn't let that happen. No matter the cost.

In my mind, Sven repeated over and over again, "*The teeth will lead* you *home*."

I was a bad person, a horrible mother, and I deserved to pay. Dane had seen fit to spare me, but I couldn't allow myself to keep hiding behind things like religion and depression. I should have acted. I should have saved my child. All those people, all those innocent lives that Dane took, they should have been me, only me. I would take Doc Morrow's advice in reverse. Instead of peace, I sought sorrow. Instead of solace, I would find pain.

I located the table of my salvation and rummaged through a box marked Hand Tools, tossing aside screwdrivers, wrenches, and ratchet bits until I finally came across the object of my desire: a pair of needle-nosed pliers.

Melissa clawed at Dane's arms while he throttled her. No blood came from the scratches, not even a whitening of the skin, for though Dane was tangible, he was not a living body.

I steeled myself, gathering every bit of gumption I had left in my person. "Dane! Let her go, you son of a bitch!"

I reviled foul language, but never before had that terminology been so apt. If ever there was a bitch in the whole wide universe, surely she was me. She was Ella May Peters, mother of Dane Peters, the Rest Stop Dentist.

Dane ignored me and continued squeezing the life from Melissa.

I reminded myself of what I was, that terrible mother who'd sat and watched her son's torture take place over the course of seventeen long, sorrowful years. I opened the pliers. I stuck one tip far back in my mouth, while the other dug up into the gums above my front teeth. I pushed hard, and blood dripped down onto my bottom lip. I closed the ends on my tooth, squeezing the handles with both hands, and shoved the tips further into my gum line. I yanked down and out.

The pain lanced up my Cupid's bow, split, zapped across my cheeks in arcing bolts, and exploded in my temples, as if someone had stabbed an ice pick into my eye. I twisted and wrenched, dug in harder, and heard the first crack. In a mouth full of saliva and blood, teeth are slippery things. The pliers faltered, but I returned to my task almost immediately. Latching back on and pulling again, I was able to extract my left front tooth. It shot from the grasp of the pliers and ricocheted around inside my mouth.

Melissa's struggling calmed. She was almost done.

The scene inside Talia's bathroom popped into my mind. I remembered how Dane had kneeled down to inspect the teeth he'd bashed from my friend's head. Then, I saw Officer Driver smashing out his own teeth before he shot himself. My mind flickered to Dane in the glow of the cruiser's overhead lights, dropping down, distracted by the teeth on the roadside.

I spit my excavated tooth onto the tile. It skittered across the floor, stopping only a foot behind Dane's prison-issue sandals.

My entire skull throbbed as if someone had set up a boom box in the center of my brain and cranked the volume on some rap song made to accompany the bouncing of a low-riding vehicle. I spat a wad of blood onto the floor in front of me. When I looked up, Dane had given up on Melissa. She lay in a pile on the floor.

He squatted and regarded the tooth with a quizzical stare. He picked it up and pinched it between his thumb and forefinger, as if testing to see if it was real.

I shoved the pliers back into my mouth, sought out one of my canines, and repeated the process. I didn't think any pain could be worse than that of the first tooth, but I was wrong. Bright, sparkling fairies dove into my vision from the corners of my sight. I ignored the brilliant-colored pixies and fought to rip a second tooth from my head.

With a painful buildup of pressure, the canine came out. The pliers held that time, and the tooth remained in the grip of the tool. I plucked the canine from the needle-nose and flicked it toward Dane. It landed two feet short of the first one.

I set about ripping out the next tooth, my remaining front one. But the pliers, slick with blood and saliva, and even my tears, would no longer hold. Or maybe my strength had left me. I didn't know for sure. I tried three times, and on each instance, they slipped.

Dane moved languidly toward the second tooth. He smiled absently as he went.

I dropped the pliers to the floor. A hammer lay among the other tools in the box. I told myself, once again, that I deserved it. Every single ounce of pain was a welcome requiem for the dead, for Dane and his victims alike.

I brandished the hammer like a sword, the claw-end pointed toward my face, and the flat, nail end aimed at Dane.

"I'm ssssssowwy, Dane," I groaned. "Ohs Lords, I'm ssssoooo sssssowwy." It was hard to talk with missing teeth, and my jaw played a bad beat in my head.

Any normal person, on any given day, might have had a survival instinct that would have made them pull the hammer at the last minute, but not me, and not then. Grinning, I swung hard, and my remaining teeth exploded. My mouth overflowed with blood. I had no way of knowing how many I'd knocked out, for my tongue found empty spaces everywhere. I spat fragments into my palm, four in all, and flicked one to the floor.

Dane followed my trail, as people had once followed his own trail of teeth. I backed up a step at a time, dropping teeth to the ground as I went until I was all out.

Spent, I dropped to my knees. Waves of pain and nausea crashed against me like waves at a buoy, and I felt myself drifting, shock taking over.

Dane, collecting my teeth as he went, came to me. He knelt down before me and put his hand, the one not holding my amateur dentistry, on my shoulder. "Ready to go home, Momma?"

I nodded. My mouth wouldn't work. My lower jaw was broken from the impact of the hammer. I could feel sections that weren't supposed to move drifting like wood under the surface of water.

Dane leaned forward and kissed my forehead.

The Lord is my shepherd. I shall not want. He makes me lie down in green pastures, He leads me beside quiet waters, He restores my soul. He guides me in paths of righteousness for His name's sake. Yea, though I walk through the valley of the shadow of death, I will fear no evil. Not my son's, nor my own.

I find myself in a field of fading greens and grays. Withered weeds rise up around me. What might have once been a stunning valley budding with life is now a desolate, dreary thing. Mountains rise at my flanks, sleeping, horn-backed monsters, awaiting the breath of life. I stand and look ahead, toward a ransacked cottage with dangling eaves that look like questioning eyebrows. The door is open, and firelight shines from within.

I walk to the cottage, but the dried creek bed behind the house catches my attention. Though no water is present, toothless faces stare up at me from piles of the dead. Victims, these people are, or were, once upon a time. Their suffering is over. Lillie Mason is there, as is a tongue-less Thomas Flynn. Fredericka Devereau in her pink sneakers and plaid Capri pants… all the others blur together. I do not know all their

257

names. Not anymore. Dead eyes watch as I return to the derelict cottage.

Sounds rise when I walk through the door, mumbling words that are nothing more than gibberish to my ears. A young version of Dane hides in one corner. He's in a fetal position, crying. To my left, Phil is crucified upon the far wall. Nails, bent down at the heads to hold him in place, jut from his wrists and feet. A crown of teeth lays askew upon his head.

"Help me," Phil pleads.

I have no voice, so I slowly shake my head.

Dane, now a grown man, suddenly stands before me. Like the child I'd seen upon entering, Dane is weeping.

I realize the boy is still in the corner. Once again, I am the fool. He's not Dane. He is Phillip. Dane has brought the boy here. Absently, I wonder where Melissa is.

Dane says, "We're all here, Momma. We're finally home."

I point at Phillip and shake my head violently. The boy is not meant to be here. If this place is meant for us, so be it, but he should let Phillip live his life.

Dane's face crinkles. He seems to consider my thoughts. "You'll stay?" he asks me.

I nod.

Dane walks to the poor boy in the corner, touches the child's shoulder, and Phillip blinks out of this world.

Dane says to me, "This isn't how I meant for this to end. All I wanted was a family. A decent family. One you never let me have. I should have just killed you and Dad."

I nod in agreement. Dane should have killed Phil and me. We had all but begged him to murder us.

On the wall, Phil thrashes. My late husband is screaming. I can now see that his mouth is devoid of teeth. He doesn't seem to notice me or Dane. He only laments. I wonder if Phil has been hanging there since he died. Dane wouldn't have cast his father into the dried creek bed. He'd want to watch the old man suffer. Endlessly.

So this will be my existence now. A purgatory of my son's design. How fitting.

Dane nails me to the wall, just like the Savior I'd put all my faith in, and I can't help but laugh. No sound comes from me, but I'm cackling all the same. If heaven or hell really do reside somewhere, I doubt I will ever see them.

When I am secured to the wall, Dane stands back to look upon his work.

"This'll do." Dane smiles. "This'll do nicely. Sing me a song, Momma."

There is but one song that fits the occasion. Finding I now have a voice, I begin, "Amazing grace, how sweet the sound, that hid a wretch like me…"

THIRTY-TWO

WHETHER THE COTTAGE IN THE valley ever really existed or not, I didn't know. But when I came back, I was in a hospital bed.

At some point, other vendors had shown up, called the proper authorities, and I was whisked away for medical treatment. The doctors reset my jaw and wired it shut. I couldn't talk, but I didn't really have much to say, so that wasn't a big deal. Everything had come to a proper close, and the Rest Stop Dentist was finally put to rest.

Surprisingly enough, a week into my hospital stay, Agent Carmine Andrews was the first person to come see me. My, but that man had aged twenty years if he'd aged a day since I saw him last. He looked like a Q-tip with his thin body and stark-white hair. He'd come to tell me what had happened, as if I hadn't been there for everything, but his story did differ quite a bit from what I'd experienced.

Andrews pulled up a chair and sat next to my hospital bed. He crossed his legs and entwined his fingers around his raised knee. "So it would seem Sven Gödel took you hostage. I know you can't talk, but you can nod. Is that correct?"

I jerked my head backward and forward.

"That's what I thought. I guess he got too close to Dane's story, went a little mad. I'm assuming he went Serial Killer Super-Fan on us. That happens a lot, actually. Maybe he saw Dane as a rock star of sorts. The writer took a great bit of notice in your son's case. I guess we know why now."

I nodded again.

"We have him on tape at a Holiday Inn, dragging you away from a murder that happened just off camera. The victim" — Andrews tapped his right cheek, just below the eye — "had a teardrop tattoo right here. Do you remember him?"

I said yes with my head.

"All right, save your neck. I can't imagine what your jaw must feel like, you nodding so much. I'm just going to run some other things by you. If you hear something wrong, you can blink several times." He uncrossed his legs and sat back in the chair. "At some point in time, Sven killed a housekeeper named Gloria Bidden. People at the hotel he was staying at said he'd been there for two weeks, but no one ever saw him coming or going. I figure Sven hunted you down after that because he felt you were unfinished business. He found you at Talia Stemsford's, murdered her, and ran off with you. You're not blinking, so I guess I'll keep on. He then killed Stanley Greatwater at your home. Shot the guy in the neck. You can tell the proper authorities why he took you back to your house after Talia's murder when your jaw heals. But I think Sven wanted to cover up any connection he had with Stanley and Officer Driver. We're guessing that the three of them meant to do you harm. Driver and Stanley spray-painted your house and harassed you a little, but Sven full-on snapped. During your road trip, Sven ditched his Mercedes in a cornfield. Yeah, we found it after the farmer who owned the land called the local PD about it. Sven bought that Nissan, the one we found in the parking lot at Happy's Flea Market. The plates match the ones caught by dashboard camera footage while Officer Driver was killing himself. I'm guessing he came after you two, possibly to avenge Stanley's death? Still can't figure out why he offed himself like he did. Nasty. You have any idea?"

I didn't know whether to blink or not, so I shook my head.

"Well, I guess we'll find out sooner or later. Or we won't. Nature of the beast, sad to say. Some mysteries"—he squinted at me—"go unsolved, unfortunately. I still can't wrap my head around Driver's death, but it happened. But what I can't figure out at all is how you acted when Sven bought the Nissan. See, I have three witnesses: Rudy Hunter and a pair of ladies that go by Adriana and Mara. The ladies say you didn't look too worried when they saw you in Rudy's parking lot, and Rudy backs that up. I'm guessing you'd settled into your fate by then. You know, they have a name for that, but I can't remember it right now. It's when a hostage falls for his or her captor. Damn, what is that called?" Agent Andrews scratched at his chin as if it would help him think. Then, he blurted, "Stockholm Syndrome! That's it. Anyway, is that what happened? I'd like to wait 'til your jaw's healed, but I want to go back to retirement someday soon. In the end, I'm guessing Sven put the pieces together concerning Melissa. Don't look so shocked. We found that interview Sven did with Dane. The disc was left inside your DVD player back at your house. None of us knew Melissa Dugan was the one who called in the info on Dane that led to his arrest until we showed up on her doorstep to warn her about Sven. All of a sudden, she couldn't wait to confess. Imagine that, having to call the police on the father of your child. Must've been rough."

I didn't dare blink.

"Let me get this one last thing straight so I can do my report. Melissa says Sven came into the flea market, guns blazing—well, one gun blazing, anyway—killing everyone in sight. As some kind of sick ode to Dane, he smashed out your teeth and broke your jaw before Melissa shot him in the head. Now, this is where I'm confused. Did he drop the gun to go after your teeth? Why didn't he just shoot you and take your teeth?"

I shrugged.

"Did you two fight? Did you wrestle the gun from his hand while he was busy threatening Melissa Dugan?"

I went ahead and nodded.

"All right. Like I said, most of this will have to be answered officially once your jaw heals, but I'm writing up my report anyway. What are they gonna do? Fire me?" Agent Andrews laughed. "I'm gonna go, but Melissa Dugan is outside with her son. She wants to talk to you. Do you feel up to it?"

I nodded.

"Okay, good. I hope they got you on some good drugs. A broken jaw is no joke. Hope you get to feeling better."

Agent Andrews got up, walked to the door, and held it open. He waved through the opening, and Melissa came in holding Phillip's hand. The boy looked well, strong, as if he'd already put the happenings at

Happy's Flea Market behind him. That was good. I didn't want to see him distraught.

Melissa motioned for him to sit in the chair Andrews had taken during our one-sided conversation. She came to my bedside and squeezed my hand.

Tears popped up in the corners of her eyes. "Thank you for what you done."

I just stared at her.

"I… I kinda lied to the cops. I can't imagine you mind that I did, but I didn't know how else to explain things. Did he find any holes in my story?"

I shook my head.

"You saved my life, Ella. And Phillip's. I would like it if you were a part of our lives. Me and Phillip. Would you like that?"

I didn't think about it, I simply nodded.

Melissa leaned in and kissed my cheek. Her face was warm against mine. "Good. I won't bother you anymore, then. Rest up. When you get out, we'll drive you home. Okay?"

I waved her off.

I was going to be able to watch Phillip grow into a man. I felt whole for the first time in my miserable existence. Life would finally right itself, and I would live out my days in peace. I just knew it.

Melissa led Phillip out, and the door closed behind them.

I settled back in the bed and cracked my knuckles.

I relaxed and thought about Phillip. No matter what body I resided in, I was still the boy's father. And my son, unlike me, would be happy.

Even if it killed him.